LIKE
THE
LION'S
TOOTH

LIKE THE LION'S TOOTH

Marjorie Kellogg

Farrar, Straus and Giroux
New York

Lines from the poem "Crazy Jane Grown Old Looks at the Dancers" reprinted with permission of Mr. M. B. Yeats and Macmillan & Co. Ltd. and the Macmillan Company (New York) from *Collected Poems* by William Butler Yeats. Copyright 1933 by The Macmillan Company, renewed 1961 by Bertha Georgie Yeats

For Richard and Angelina, with love

I found that ivory image there
Dancing with her chosen youth,
But when he wound her coal-black hair
As though to strangle her, no scream
Or bodily movement did I dare,
Eyes under eyelids did so gleam;
Love is like the lion's tooth.

W. B. Yeats
"Crazy Jane Grown Old
Looks at the Dancers"

LIKE
THE
LION'S
TOOTH

■   ■   ■   ■

THE DAY SHE DIDN'T COME FOR HIM, BEN waited an hour in the reception hall, then he went down by the river, taking his suitcase with him, being careful not to get his shoes muddy, watching that the brambles didn't tear his new suit, trying not to sweat and mess himself up. He stayed there until after dark watching the boats, trying to make out the voices—voices shouted over the sound of outboard motors. It was the Fourth of July. From the riverbank he could see the tracks of the

New York Central, and he threw rocks on the tracks, hoping he would derail a fast-moving passenger train and kill everybody aboard. In his mind he saw the bloody bodies littered along the tracks, arms and legs torn from their sockets and strewn in the bushes down by the water. Their wallets would be scattered too, and since they would be dead and wouldn't need it any more, Ben would gather up the money—more than usual because of the Fourth—and get the hell out of this place. He was eleven.

At one in the morning, Ben climbed a tree and tied his suitcase to one of the high branches. Then he walked along the tracks to the station, where he boarded a train bound for New York City. By the time the conductor found he had no ticket, the train was already in the tunnel leading to Grand Central Station. The big station was almost empty, and he sat on one of the benches making his plan. This time he would find him and drive an ice pick through his eardrum. This time he would run a razor down his spine and lift out his backbone like you would a fish spine and throw it in the garbage.

It was nine in the morning before he got to Brooklyn. In the daylight, his feelings were thinned by the problems of traveling without money, eating without money, remembering an address that, when he lived there, he thought he would remember a lifetime. He wished now he had taken more care of the suit when he climbed the tree and rode the train. She would like to see him in a new suit, light blue and with nice wide shoulders. He could easily pass for fifteen, he thought, if he didn't hunch, if he took bigger steps. He would lie and tell her he had a job. The prosperous son. The new suit was part of it. She could buy him a tie, if she wanted.

He came out of the subway into the light. The apartment could not be more than two blocks away, because when he lived there, they walked to meet her at the subway every night at 9:25. They would line up on the steps, all five of them, first Ray, then Carol Ann, then him, then Philip, then Winnie, in the order of their age because they figured it was cuter that way. They had seen something like it in a movie. Or they would hide behind the trash cans at the top of the stairs, watching her face grow anxious as she looked for them. "Surprise!" She would manage a laugh.

Ben could see them now, as if he were standing away: Ray always next to her, reporting, telling on them, pretending to be the man. Philip hanging back, sucking on his fingers. The girls dancing backwards. "Mama, Mama, Ray's a liar!" Winnie chanted. Every night the same. He himself standing away, waiting for her to smile at him over the heads of the others.

He turned left at the corner. The apartment was on the fifth floor under the roof. There was no bell. There was no lock on the downstairs door. He went up the stairs two at a time, seeing old landmarks: a dark spot on the wall where Mrs. Ruiz had thrown a pot of boiling beans at Mr. Ruiz; a word he himself had written with the remains of an aerosol can. Outside of the apartment he stopped to arrange the scene in his mind. They would be sitting at the table eating cornflakes and bananas. I missed the train, she would say. That's why I didn't come for you, honest-to-God. Winnie, say hello to your brother. They were surely all of them there. He banged on the door with his fist. Maybe they were asleep, he thought. The Fourth of July, they would sleep late. He banged harder.

A woman in a nightgown wearing thick spectacles opened the door and looked at him down the long plane of her nose.

"Yes?" she said, "yes?"

■　■　■　■

HE KEPT THINKING OF PHILIP AS HE WENT through the streets looking for her, as if one disaster would nullify another. The wind was blowing that night, whining around the base of the tower. That's why he could not hear what Philip was saying.

"When did you see her last?"

"A month ago."

"Oh well then," the vegetable man said, dismissing it as if a month were an eternity.

Philip sucking on his fingers, too skinny, too pale.

"Was she redheaded?"

"Yes. That's her."

"She hasn't been around for weeks. You a friend of hers?"

A friend of hers? The thought astonished him. What the hell did this man have in mind?

He finally went to the graveyard to think. He sat on Elizabeth Addison's grave and tried to put Philip out of his mind and figure out where his mother had gone. But he found it hard to concentrate on the problem. He was distracted by a truck rumbling over the cobblestones, by a man placing a flag on a nearby grave. He tried to force his thoughts back to her by remembering the places they had lived: Manhattan, Queens, Mt. Vernon, as if her whereabouts now would magically fall into the sequence. It didn't work. One stairwell melted into the next. He forgot the color of her eyes, the shape of her hands. Philip keep reappearing anyway. Finally he had to admit that his father must have come back and found her.

Ben took a black marking pencil out of his pocket.

Fuck you Elizabeth Addison, he wrote on the gravestone.

■ ■ ■ ■

MADELINE FOUND HIM DOWN BY THE TRACKS, lying in the brush with a deep wound in the side of his head. Flies had settled in the wound—that was how she knew he had been there for a while. He was wearing the new light blue suit he was to have gone home in, but the jacket was split down the back center seam and the pants were encrusted with mud. That Fourth of July weekend there had been severe thunderstorms.

The previous fall, shortly after he had come to the School, Madeline had taken him over, deciding that what he needed was someone to look after him. She sat him down on the steps of the cottage and cleaned his fingernails. Then she cut his toenails with a pair of garden shears she had stolen from the greenhouse. When she threatened to take the wax out of his ears, he put a stop to it.

"Jesus Christ," he said, smiling at her.

"I'm going into town," Madeline said. "Want to come?"

"No."

"I want you to," she said, clearing a booger out of his nose.

"O.K.," he said.

She tended to boss him, but he didn't mind.

They went over the back fence to avoid the hassle of

asking permission. She was fifteen and taller than he, a big girl with white, fat, misshapen arms and legs, but a pretty face and wide blue eyes.

"Where are we going?" he said.

"To Grant's. I need a new brassière."

The manager of Grant's saw them come in and he and the three clerks kept them under constant surveillance. Of all the kids who shoplifted, the ones from the School were the worst.

They walked slowly up and down the aisles holding hands, the manager following three feet behind. When they left, he sighed.

"You got to stick to them like ticks," he said to the clerks. "Otherwise, they walk out with the store."

Ben and Madeline did not look at each other until they were in the shack they had built from a piano crate near the river. They closed the door of the shack behind them and emptied their pockets into Madeline's skirt: two brassières, a bottle of Midnight in Paris, a pair of wire cutters, and three ballpoint pens.

"My little boy must be tired," Madeline said. He lay down beside her and closed his eyes.

"And hungry," she said, opening her blouse.

He nodded and she held the back of his head.

She thought he looked a little pale and she reminded herself to start him on the one-a-day vitamin pills she had stolen from the drugstore.

■ ■ ■ ■

IN THE OLD DAYS, WHEN THEY WERE ALL TO-
gether, before his father went to sea, and was sober and
not accusing his mother of anything, they sometimes
took a picnic out to Long Beach and sat in the shade
under the boardwalk. They were all fair and sunburned
easily, all except Ben, who turned chocolate brown, and
it was rare that their mother would even let them take
off their shirts.

His old man would prop himself against a piling and
sleep away the afternoon, and Sara, his mother, would
sit looking out to sea, letting the sand sift through her
fingers. Sometimes she would let Ben cover her with sand
with only her head sticking out, and then he would
decorate her with shells and seaweed and any other
bright-colored trash he could find on the beach.

"I look like a birthday cake," Sara would say, smiling
at his nonsense.

At the beach he always felt free and light on his feet.
He would run and belly-dive the waves and swim out
beyond the buoy until the people on the beach looked
like black dots. Going out, he would swim on his back
as though the sight of the beach were his anchor line.

"I was watching you," Sara would say. He would
swell with pride.

At the beach, Philip played in the shade, digging

quietly among the pilings, finding things everyone else had overlooked.

"Why don't you go in the water?" his mother would say. "Go on, Philly. It will do you good." Philip would never even look up. His mind was considering a rusty bracelet with blue and red stones.

When it was dark, they would gather up things for the trip home. Ben hated this time. Just once he wanted to stay until everyone had gone, when the beach was deserted.

"Daddy, Daddy," Winnie would shriek, "I can't *see!*" The pilings under the boardwalk looked like giants in the dark.

"Open your eyes, then," he would grumble.

"They *are* open, they *are!*" And she would tug at his pants until he would pick her up and carry her out to the street on his shoulders. From a distance, they all looked very happy.

■　■　■　■

MADELINE GOT HIM OUT OF BED AT THREE IN the morning to tell him that the girls in Swanson Cottage were rioting and did he want to watch. He grinned at her for knowing him so well.

"It's really wild," she said. He took her hand, which was already sweaty with excitement.

Swanson Cottage housed the twelve- to fourteen-year-old girls and was thought by the staff to be the toughest to manage. The eyes of these children were glazed with neglect and cruelty, which they had not yet learned to hide.

"We can watch from under the stairs," Madeline whispered.

When Ben saw them, he began to laugh. There were fifteen of them, and they were rioting all right, but without making a sound. They had scissors and razor blades with which they slashed the pillows and the drapes and the upholstered furniture, all of which had been installed two weeks before by the decorating committee of the School's board of directors. And they had cans of red paint and they were writing such things as *Mr Rose is a whore* over the new green and white eighteenth-century-motif wallpaper which the decorating committee had chosen with the idea of instilling a bit of subliminal culture into this hornet's nest.

When Ben laughed, Julie Williams came over to him and put her face within an inch of his.

"You shut up," she hissed, "or we'll cut you up with the other shit." He could smell her anger.

The riot had been planned with the skill of a major general. Julie drilled them sometimes until two in the morning, going back and forth from the three dormitory rooms, waking them out of their sleep and punishing them severely for any lapse in discipline. The goal was silence.

"Otherwise," Julie said, "they'll call the shitty police." Julie seldom spoke without making some reference to excrement.

"The first person to laugh will get the crap knocked out of him," she whispered in the dark dormitory as they began the silence drills. Then she would tell them dirty stories to try to make them laugh, or she would tickle them, and if they made a sound, she would hit them in the mouth with her open hand, or she would pull their hair or pinch the tender insides of their legs. Down the rows of beds she went, dressed in tight corduroy pants and a frayed Oxford cloth shirt which hung below her knees.

Little Jane O'Connor, who was subject to nervous bursts of crying, was told she would have to stay in bed during the riot with the others Julie had eliminated (Melba, who was a born tattletale, and Baby Frances, who was too vague and impulsive to train). Little Jane cried all the harder at being excluded, but Julie was adamant: "One rotten troop will crap up the whole platoon."

In the center of the riot sat Mrs. Meredith. She held her head to one side as if she had an earache, and the tears washed down over her white-powdered cheeks. Mrs. Meredith hated Swanson Cottage and she hated its tough, unruly girls. I am a gentlewoman, she would say to herself from time to time, rolling the sentence over in her mouth as if it were a candy. She would never forgive her husband for dying and leaving her with practically no resources but to work in this place.

Ben went over and sat on the floor beside Mrs. Meredith.

"They're sure wrecking the joint," he said pleasantly.

For a moment, her face lit up. "Will you run and get Mr. Rose?" she said.

Ben shook his head. "I'm sorry, I couldn't do that."

"Why not?" she said. "Are you afraid of Miss Julie Williams?"

Ben smiled. "No."

"Then stop them," she said. "They'll listen to their own kind."

"It's just furniture," Ben said, patting her arm. "Why don't you go down to the kitchen and make an apple cobbler. When they finish here, they'll be starved."

She looked at him as if he had dropped from another planet.

"You ought to be sent away, all of you!" she shouted, unable to contain herself any longer.

"We have been," Ben said.

■ ■ ■ ■

"IF ANYBODY ASKS WHERE YOUR MAMA IS, just point and keep going."

Winnie giggled. "Point where?" she said.

"Anywhere," Ray said. "And don't cry, no matter who says what."

"I won't," Winnie said. Already her eyes were brimming at the thought.

"Don't cry!" Ray shouted, shaking her until her teeth rattled.

Although their mother told them to stay at home while she was away working, they never did. As soon as she had gone, they packed the lunch she had left in the refrigerator and decided where they would go. Ben always voted for the beach and Winnie for the movies, but most of the time they were outvoted, because Philip never voted for anything and Carol Ann would always side with Ray. So they went where Carol Ann and Ray wanted to go.

That summer they traveled without money, finding the dim subway entrances where the changemaker was busy reading, or getting on exit doors of crowded busses.

On cool days they would walk across the Brooklyn Bridge and look at the ships and then take a subway on the Manhattan side, usually as far as Times Square. Sometimes Winnie would get the giggles in the subway and wet her pants, or Carol Ann would get a headache from not eating.

"I'm too damned hungry to go on," Carol Ann would say in her tough, boy's voice. And they would have to eat lunch then and there, regardless of where they were.

Or Philip would lag so far behind, contemplating something in a corner of a store window, or some junk in the gutter, that they would have to wait. Ben would go back for him.

"Come on, honey," he would say, and Philip would smile and take Ben's hand. Philip smiled only at Ben.

"Why the hell do you call him honey?" Carol Ann demanded. "Honey is for girls, if you must use such a dumb expression."

That summer they went mostly to cool museums. They looked at paintings in huge gold frames. They stared at mobiles and tall thin statues in graveled gardens; at a simulated eclipse of the moon. They gazed at mummies, and, cage by cage, every animal in three zoos. At the places that charged admission, they lined up and entered with the day campers, who came by the bus-loads. Or they pretended to the guard that they had already been inside but had left someone behind. At this, Winnie would begin to cry, even though she knew it was a made-up story, and the guard would let them through the gate, his heart full for the unhappy little girl.

Inevitably, Carol Ann would sum up for them on the

way home—like an official guide: "Well, *that* was a bust!" she would say, or "We'll come back *here* next week."

Going home, Philip would fall asleep with his head on Ben's shoulder. Ben would check now and then to make sure he was still breathing.

■　■　■　■

STEVE WAS A LITTLE MAN. HIPS AS NARROW as tweezers. He took Ben into the bedroom and closed the door. There was no sound but the radiator spitting in the corner. Ben closed his eyes and listened to the radiator and hoped that this time he would faint.

Outside there was two feet of snow on the ground and it was still coming down. The rest of them sat around the kitchen table looking at their hands. Except Philip. He stood by the window watching the snow-flakes slant across the bright cone of light from the street lamp and disappear into the dark.

"You never learn, do you?" Steve was saying. He spoke in a whisper, without rancor. "You never learn that when I come home I like to find my little family where I left them. Is that an unreasonable request?" He took a piece of clothesline from his pocket and tied Ben's hands above his head to the bed.

"Well, is it?" he said, holding Ben's face in his hands.

"No."

In the street, a car engine turned again and again against the cold, trying to start. From the snow-reflected light outside, Ben tried to see his father's face, but there was only the outline of his head against the window.

"So what happens?" Steve said, slipping off Ben's pants and folding them neatly. "So I run all the way home from the ship and bingo, my little family has gone away and left me. Zip zip, gone like thieves in the night." Steve put the pants on a chair and smoothed out a final wrinkle.

"And who planned it all? Who convinced my little family to pick up stakes?" He ran his hand lightly over Ben's belly.

"My second son, Benjamin. Yessir. Would you believe that?"

The battery is dying, Ben thought. That's why the car won't start. He heard the car door slam and a man swear.

"In Japan there is a special kind of punishment for little boys who hide their families while their fathers are at sea. Do you know what they do to them?"

From the river came the sound of a freighter picking its way upstream through the storm.

"In Japan, they insert a piece of metal into the boy's rectum—" He hesitated, musing, as though some detail had escaped him.

The freighter whistled again. Ben wondered if the captain knew enough to avoid the currents at the base of the bridge.

"Tell me, Ben." His father had pulled himself back into the present. "Why do you hate me so?"

"Because you are a rotten, lousy bastard," Ben whispered.

"Is that so?" Steve said. He got slowly on top of Ben and began.

■ ■ ■ ■

THAT NIGHT HIS MOTHER CALLED THE POLICE. Two of them came and ambled slowly around the apartment, poking at the furniture with their night sticks as if they were looking for a bomb.

"So what's the problem?" one of them said finally.

"I was beating the kid," Steve said amiably. "I admit it."

The cops made Ben take off his shirt. They examined his skin and they looked into his mouth and, for some reason, at the bottoms of his feet.

"Apparently not very hard," one of the cops said, smiling.

Steve shrugged. "I found out he stole cigarettes out of the A & P."

"Yeah?" the cop said. Then he asked Sara if she wanted to press charges against her husband.

Sara looked at Steve and he smiled back ruefully—the look of a father who was only doing his job.

"I guess not," Sara said.

"If you want my opinion," the cop said to her, "be glad he cares enough to discipline the kid."

When they left, Steve hit his wife so hard on the side of the head that he knocked her off the chair. Ray tried to intervene and the little girls screamed until they were breathless. Philip stood unmoving by the window, watching the snow fall.

About a week after the police came, his father went back to sea, shipping this time on a tanker. He was to be gone three months. The next day, while they were eating supper, Sara told them they would be moving to Brooklyn.

"Why, may I ask, are we going to Brooklyn?" Carol Ann said.

"Why not?" Ray said. Ray was flunking the eighth grade and glad to get out.

"I love Brooklyn," Winnie said.

"Now how the hell do you know?" Carol Ann said. "You've never been there."

Ben looked at his mother. "He will find us there," he said.

"Not this time," Sara said. She put her arm around Ben's shoulder and drew him close to her. "This time," she said to all of them, "you're not to tell any of your friends where we are going. Is that clear?" They nodded solemnly—except Winnie. She wiggled in her seat and mushed her peas into her mashed potatoes and looked as if she were going to cry.

"I mean it, Winnie," their mother said.

"I'm going to tell Billy Behrens where we're going," Winnie said.

"No one!" Sara said, shaking Winnie's arm.

"Yes I am, I am!" Winnie wailed. "He's in love with me."

"In *love* with you!" Carol Ann exploded. "How the hell could he be in love with you? You're only five years old!"

"He is, he is!" The tears fell freely into Winnie's plate and she stirred them in with the peas and potatoes.

"May I ask how old Billy Behrens is?" Carol Ann said. "Twenty-seven?"

■ ■ ■ ■

THEY MOVED TO DEAN STREET ON A GRAY DAY in March. A sharp wind threatened to bring the storm which had already crippled Washington and Philadelphia. Sara prayed the moving company would not hear the weather report. They had, but they came anyway—

three old men in a red and orange van whose age gave it a comic, down-at-the-heels look. The old men needed the business.

Ben packed his things in a cardboard box, his clothes first, then a leather bag with marbles which he hadn't opened in years, a jigsaw puzzle of an Alpine scene, a small rusted replica of the Statue of Liberty. There had been other things to pack, but he had thrown them out, into the incinerator before Philip could get to them. Then he stood by the window and watched the water swirl at the base of the George Washington Bridge, trying to plant it hard in his mind so that he would not forget it.

For three hours the old men grunted and groaned up and down the four flights carrying out the faded furniture and the cardboard cartons which younger men could have loaded in an hour. But they were kindly, and in the end they agreed to let Sara and the children ride along in the van. The snow had started.

Winnie and Carol Ann sat on the sofa and played cards as though they were sitting in the living room. Ray rode in front with the movers and Philip fell asleep behind a carton of dishes. Sara sat in the upholstered chair, her head in her hands, the collar of her coat turned up against the cold.

Ben listened to the grinding of the gears. Maybe the old men were dumb enough to take the wrong turn and end up going west over the George Washington Bridge. To Lost Mountain, Wyoming. He could get a job there, in Lost Mountain, he thought. He and Ray. They could all change their names.

Philip cried out.

"Shut up, honey," Ben said, pulling him into his lap. Philip smiled and hid his face under Ben's arm.

"Three no-trump," Winnie said.

"May I ask how you can bid three no-trump without a single solitary honor in your hand?" Carol Ann said.

"Mommie, Carol Ann is cheating, cheating! Yes she is!"

■   ■   ■   ■

MR. ROONEY, THE SCHOOL PSYCHOLOGIST, felt that the riot was the result of mounting sexual tensions among the girls at Swanson Cottage and, as such, was perfectly normal. He explained this at a staff meeting called to discuss the matter, adding that he planned to see the girls in individual, therapeutic sessions to give them further opportunity to ventilate. Mr. Rose, the director, made a note of this, but he could not for the life of him decide how to explain the disaster to the decorating committee of the board. Mr. Ferguson, the gardener, who also attended the staff meetings, shook his head as he left the meeting. He walked slowly down to his greenhouse and remained there the rest of the afternoon, brooding on why such a thing should happen, and unable to concentrate on the tomato seedlings which needed thinning. He had long before given up trying to understand the behavior of the children. He knew only that they came from homes where the parents mistreated them or the father was gone or the mother was drunk or a prostitute or all these things. To him, this was enough to explain why they did what they did—why they stole things out of his greenhouse, why they lied and set fires and wrote filthy words on the sides of the buildings. What to do about it was something else. At one of the first staff meetings he was invited to attend, he had been asked to state his views on a similar incident. "I would thrash them," he had said. In their patient, college voices, the other staff members told him why this would not be acceptable.

"I would thrash them too," his wife had said that night. She was making a seven-minute icing in a double boiler with an electric beater. She loved her husband's accounts of the children's mischief, particularly if they were sexual or offbeat in nature.

"I would thrash them and show them who's boss and then I'd lock them in a closet and see how they liked *that!*" She turned the icing out on the cake, making swirls like whitecaps on the ocean waves, pausing now and then to lick the beater and admire her work.

"I wouldn't go that far," said her husband.

■ ■ ■ ■

PHILIP WORE A BLUE SHIRT THAT DAY, AND
sneakers with knotted laces. No coat. No socks. He
shivered like a thin old animal. *Come down from there,
honey!* Ben heard his own voice drift off on the wind.

■ ■ ■ ■

JULIE WILLIAMS HUNG HER LEGS OVER THE
chair arm and stared out of the window at the Day Liner
on its way up the Hudson River. It was a clear day and
she could almost see the faces of the passengers as they
gathered along the rail and in the bow of the boat.
Johnneeeeeeee! A voice floated over the water as though
it were coming from the next cottage. Johneeeeeeeee!
On their way to Bear Mountain, Julie thought. Rotten
bastards.

"You can trust me," Mr. Rooney was saying. He
spoke slowly and clearly as if Julie were a foreigner.
"I'll bet you didn't know that."

Julie gave a short laugh and made her hands into
binoculars.

"What are you looking at?" Rooney said, trying to
approximate her gaze. Julie stood up, blocking his view.

It was her boat and she intended to keep it that way until it slipped from sight. Her hands, with their invisible lenses, seemed to bring the people closer. She saw that some of them had picnic lunches spread out on their laps, and that the children were wearing shorts and sneakers and drinking Coke. She was about to give up on the boat and let it sail off on its dumb trip up the river with its stupid, overfed passengers, when she saw the Man. He was sitting alone on the stern on a camp stool, his hands folded across his chest, staring down at the flat rippling wake. The sight of him made her throat knot, and she gasped for air as if she were choking.

"What's the matter?" Rooney said, and she kicked at him to try to silence him, as if the sound of his voice interfered with what she was seeing.

The Man was wearing a yellow shirt and a canvas hat pulled over his eyes, but there was no mistaking who he was. Without thinking, Julie called to him, but in the middle of the first syllable she hesitated, as though she had forgotten his name. The sound she made was like a howl, a syllable flattened at the end, in the back of her throat. It startled Rooney, this strange animal cry, and he jumped up from his desk and put a protective hand on her shoulder.

"Get your friggin hands off me!" She turned and spat the words in his face. He had forgotten that nobody ever touched Julie Williams.

When she looked back to the river, the boat was gone and the man on the deck was gone and there was only the flat ripple of the wake.

"Now look what you did, you goddamned honey-sucking bastard!" She took a swing at him as she started out the door, knocking his glasses to the floor.

"Where are you going?" His voice was as plaintive as a child's. Something in the sound of it and in the sight of him for the first time with his eyes naked made her pause.

"To Bear Mountain," she said, as though her answer were an apology.

■ ■ ■ ■

ON DEAN STREET IN BROOKLYN THEY HAD two unconnected rooms which opened into a dark hallway. Sara made one of them into a sitting room-dining room-bedroom for herself and the girls, and the boys slept in the other room. She cooked their meals on a hot plate in the hall shared by three other families. They all used a common toilet. Ben would remember the stink of the place for years: cooking oil and urine and the sweet rot of garbage. They stayed there until June, when Philip was bitten in the mouth by a rat.

That June night, late, the boys were in their room—
their apartment, as they liked to think it—separated from
the giggling girls and the watchful eye of their mother.
They locked the door and tapped on the wall to signify
to her that they were in bed. Then Ray and Ben sat by
the window looking into the street, listening to the music
the Puerto Ricans played from the steps across the
street. Ray lit a cigarette for each of them, and they
smoked like men, dragging the smoke deep into their
lungs, cupping the cigarettes in their hands, serious and
watchful of each other.

"I wish I had a bottle of beer," Ray said.

They heard Philip make a noise from the bed, but that
was not unusual. Philip seldom spoke in words anybody
could understand and this particular sound did not alarm
them. In the street another guitarist joined those already
on the stoop and they played a plaintive island song har-
monizing in soft thirds, stringing out the notes until they
disappeared into the sounds of the dark street.

When they had finished their cigarettes, they lay down
on the bed and looked at the ceiling. Ray was on his
usual subject: where he would go when he ran away.
Ben only half listened. The other half of him always
listened for the sound of his father's step on the stair.

In the night, Ben was awakened by the feel of something sticky on his chest. He found Philip asleep there,
which was not unusual, and for a moment he thought it
was only warm drool from Philip's mouth. But his mind

would not let it go at that, and finally he got up and put on the light.

What he saw made him swear in fear.

"Oh shit," he said, jumping up and down as though the floor were covered with broken glass. His chest was dripping with blood. "Oh shit, Ray! Mama!" He danced up and down, afraid to touch the blood. Then he saw Philip's face. Philip's bottom lip was the size of an apple, a deep purple apple with a bite taken out of it, and he was trying to smile at Ben, who was still dancing and swearing. The little boy held his head to one side as if the weight of his swollen lip were too much for his neck to support. He looked at Ben and tried to smile, and with this Ben broke into a laugh. Ray went and got Sara, and when they came back, Ben was holding Philip and Ben was choking with laughter, but with no fun in it, and Philip was still trying to smile over his monstrous lip.

■ ■ ■ ■

JULIE WILLIAMS RAN ACROSS THE SCHOOL yard and out of the gate toward town, her head down like an angry pony. Mr. Ferguson looked up from a border of marigolds. No good, no good, he thought, not knowing what he meant, but guessing the judgment had been transplanted from his wife. There was no doubt that Julie Williams could run—like himself fifty years before, and for a second, watching her, he felt the old joy of that special freedom.

She passed Ben and Madeline on their way back from town and they turned to admire her.

"She's after him again," Madeline said.

"Do you think she'll ever catch him?" Ben said.

"I don't know."

She ran through the town, through the red lights, causing a minor accident at the main intersection, causing the cop to blast his whistle at her, causing the A & P supply trucker to lose a few years off the end of his life for almost hitting a child, causing Mrs. Meredith, the cottage mother, who saw Julie race by while she was buying a box of rouge at the five-and-ten, to curse her dead husband again. What would she tell Mr. Rose this time? That she was still incapable of handling Miss Julie Williams? Love and kindness are not working, Mr. Rose!

She did not stop until she got to the Parkway. And after crossing over, she planted herself directly in the middle of the northbound lanes, causing four cars almost to collide. The drivers of all four cars got out and approached her carefully, their anger masked by fear and curiosity, while the traffic backed up behind them. What was a child doing in the middle of the Parkway in corduroy pants and a man's shirt, the sweat pouring off her small black face, breathing like a winded dog?

"I got to get to Bear Mountain," she said.

Bear Mountain! Their anger, their incredulity bounced like stones on the pavement. Do you realize that you almost—

"I was with my scout troop," she said, "and they went off without me."

Ah, so she had not escaped from a loony bin after all. She was with an organized group of girls her own age. All of them sane. Why did they leave you, honey? The horns were blasting for a mile down the road.

"I got out to pee-pee . . . and—" she dropped her eyes and forced her lip to tremble—"and I guess I got lost in the bushes."

There were ten or so of them now, and they all broke into good-natured laughter. She had to *what?* someone down the road asked. Pee-pee! a man shouted, pee-pee! They drove off and left her, poor little thing. Come on, I'll take you to Bear Mountain. No, *I'm* going right there. So am I! You come with *me*.

Julie Williams was at Bear Mountain in forty minutes, well ahead of the boat.

The Man did not come down the gangplank. No man in a yellow shirt and a canvas hat, or in either one, for that matter.

She went aboard and searched the boat, thinking that perhaps he had decided to stay and sun himself on the rear deck, but he was not there, and apparently he had taken the chair with him too. She looked in all the likely places, even the men's toilets, and when the boat finally left and she still did not see him, she rode back to New York on it, thinking that he would have to show up eventually. When the boat docked in Manhattan, she stood by the gangplank again, looking into the face of every passenger, in the event she had missed him. When he did not appear, she decided he had seen her and deliberately eluded her and gone to Times Square to look at the freaks. She followed him there, dogtrotting all the way across Forty-second Street without a pause.

■　■　■　■

LIKE THE PRELUDE TO A SEIZURE, BEN COULD sense when his father was to return. It was as though they were connected by an instinct of the primal world which drove the man to appear on a certain date and the boy to be expecting him.

They moved from Dean Street to a fifth-floor walk-up near Jamaica Avenue the day after Philip was bitten by the rat. It was a palace, with two bedrooms and a sit-in kitchen and windows which let in the sun. Sara found a job in Manhattan and she left them alone that summer, putting their lunch in the refrigerator. You stay in the house, she would say, knowing they wouldn't. Or you go play in the cemetery. It's cool there, and there's no traffic. They declined her advice and that was the summer they toured the city, museum by museum, and zoo by zoo.

Ben was the only one of them who went to the cemetery. Winnie was afraid to go, afraid a bony hand would reach out from a grave and grab her. Carol Ann had other reasons.

"It's morbid," she would say, proud to know such a stunning word. "Why anybody would want to spend time in such a *morbid* place as that . . ."

But Ben liked to roam among the dead: Edward Finney 1891–1935, probably double pneumonia; the McMurtry clan, husband, wife, and three children, undoubtedly a fire; and Elizabeth Addison, his favorite dead old lady, lying there with her rings and bracelets and her long hair growing longer. Elizabeth Addison, killed in a crash, carted away with the rest of the trash . . .

The mother's efforts to hide the tracks of herself and her children were futile. She always left behind some clue, some shred of her scent which he eventually came across. Her problem was that she had never seriously thought of what her life would be like without him.

■　■　■　■

JULIE WILLIAMS FOUND THE MAN IN TIMES
Square. He was playing a pinball machine in an arcade
with the deftness of a pro, keeping the machine in deli-
cate imbalance with his hip. She noted, however, that he
had found time to change his shirt and hat. As a matter
of fact, he was wearing a plaid summer jacket over a
T-shirt, and a baseball cap with *Mets* written across the
crown. If he thought this disguise fooled her, he was
dead wrong. She took up a post just inside the archway,
and pretended she was waiting for someone. Every so
often, she would steal a glance at him, not letting him
become aware of her presence. She had learned a great
deal about tracking in the years she had been looking
for him. For one thing, you never follow too close. You
never look too long because the person you are looking
at begins to sense it and grows uneasy. And you never
speak, because your voice is a dead giveaway. As to the
not speaking, Julie was the silence expert of the age.
Hadn't she just conducted a silent riot?

The Man put in another coin, but before he began to
play, he stretched his arm over his head to ease the
muscle tension, and while he was doing this, he turned
and looked out through the archway to the street. It was
him, all right, Julie said to herself. She could tell even
though he had grown a moustache.

Julie looked down the sidewalk for the friend she was

pretending to meet. She yawned casually, as someone would do who is bored and waiting. Then she pulled a piece of cuticle from the index finger of her left hand. While she was doing this, a group of kids stormed into the place and set the machines going. One of the boys approached her and bumped her with his hip.

"Baby, baby," he said to her, bumping her again, "what you doing so far from home?"

"Bug off," she said to him.

The boy laughed. He was over six feet and he wore an orange undershirt and purple striped pants. He leaned over her, making an arch of his arms.

"For you, anything," he said.

Julie tried to duck under his arms, but he lowered them, trapping her.

"Ta ta ta ta," he said, as if he were scolding a child.

Suddenly Julie realized that she had lost sight of the Man at the pinball machine.

"Let me go," Julie hissed at the boy, but he only moved closer. He was holding her now with his body, backing her head into the wall with his chest. The bells on the machines exploded around her.

"What's your name?" the boy was saying.

But the Man was gone and this was the only thing that mattered to her now. She clawed the boy with such fury that he backed away in pain and amazement. And she ran so fast up the street, convinced that the Man had gone north on Eighth Avenue, that when the boy turned to look after her, only seconds later, she had completely disappeared.

"Man, did you see that?" the boy said to his friend.

■ ■ ■ ■

IT HAD BEEN CAROL ANN'S IDEA TO GO TO THE Botanical Gardens in the Bronx. The orchids will be "gorgeous," she said, using another one of her fancy words. But the trouble was, it had been an idea in transit and they were already on the West Side of Manhattan, heading for their sixth trip to the Planetarium.

"I feel like a change," she announced, and although Ben fought with her and called her a whore-bitch for bossing them around, they proceeded to the Bronx.

"You're worse than she is," Ben said to Ray, "like a damned pansy bossed around by that creep!" With this, Ray grabbed Ben's arm and twisted it painfully behind his back. Ray was a mild, pale boy, but he was tall and he held Ben against the door of the subway until it came to the next stop.

At the Botanical Gardens, Winnie first threw up in the tropical plants and then she began to cry because the orchids looked to her like spiders. And besides, she wailed, how could they be orchids without purple ribbon?

It was such a long trip home that they ended up being caught in the rush hour, and while it was easier to travel without money, it was harder to stay together, and somewhere between 149th Street and Times Square, they lost Ben. Ray decided that they must go on without him, that Ben could make it on his own.

Ben had deliberately gotten himself separated from them in the subway. First he transferred Philip's hand, which he had been holding, into Ray's. Philip looked at him and smiled, so knowingly that for a second Ben was afraid Philip had seen through the bones of his head into his thoughts. Then at the 96th Street stop Ben slipped through the churning crowd and crossed over to the uptown side, where he caught the train to 168th Street. He was tired of them, particularly Carol Ann, who was getting more and more on his nerves, running them all over town like a bunch of sheep, deciding everything. At one point, as they walked toward the gate of the Botanical Gardens, he had seen the profile of her face, not that of a twelve-year-old, but of a middle-aged woman, tense and drawn with the struggle of maintaining control. He had added glasses to the profile and put her into a house dress instead of jeans and there she was, thirty-seven years old, nagging at her kids and worrying about the rent. He had had to look away.

At 168th Street, he started toward the river. They had lived in this neighborhood for a while, but now it seemed different, as though the buildings had been rearranged—

the same buildings, but put on different streets—streets where he had lived even before that. So his sister was an old woman of thirty-seven and now the streets had become other streets. It couldn't be helped. He had come uptown, he thought, to look at the George Washington Bridge, to walk by the river under the great gray stanchion and watch the water eddy at the base. He walked along 168th Street, caught in the crowd of people leaving the buildings of the Medical Center which surrounded him, hurrying home. *They* should be home now, he thought, in the kitchen, wondering where he was. Winnie would be crying.

At Fort Washington Avenue he could see across to the Palisades, where gray clouds of a storm were brewing. Well, they had never gotten to Lost Mountain, Wyoming. Those old men in the red and orange van had been too smart to make that kind of a mistake.

When he got to Riverside Drive, the river was raked with whitecaps. He knew it would be a matter of minutes before the rain came, and he thought it was for that reason that he turned back and ran all the way to the subway. Actually, the first ring of fear, which had to do with the arrival of his father, was around him. And he could only run head-on into the center of it.

■ ■ ■ ■

WHERE DID YOU GO, PHILIP? I CAN NEVER
keep track of you. Did someone chase him there, or had
he seen a piece of junk shining from an arm of the tower?
He was like a little shiner left on the riverbank by a
falling tide, flapping around with nothing to breathe.

■ ■ ■ ■

THE RAIN BEAT DOWN ON THE DOCK, OBSCUR-
ing everything except the forwardmost part of the bow
of the ship, *The American Falcon*, her lines slack, the
black river water slapping at her scummy sides. The man
rolled a T-shirt and stuffed it into the duffel, a mechan-
ical act and one of the last he had to complete before
leaving the ship.

He threw his bag on his shoulder, and saying goodbye
to no one, he came down the gangplank as quiet as a cat,
his small form almost invisible against the sky. The wind
had begun on the river, harder now, rocking the ship
gently from stern to stem, sending the waves scudding
up toward the George Washington Bridge. Home.
Home from the sea.

On West Street, in the forest of beams under the

highway, he broke into a trot, head bent against the rain, the duffel riding like a natural hump on his back. The bar he knew near Fourteenth Street was closed, burned out by a fire and boarded over. *Manny's Way*. The sign was licked by smoke. Anyone trapped in that fire would have been crisped like a French fried onion from the layers of grease on the walls and windows. Too bad, it was a good bar.

He turned east on Fourteenth Street. In the wholesale-meat district, one warehouse was open. Strange, at this hour, he thought. At the curb, a Cadillac with its motor idling, wipers whispering against the rain. The door of the narrow warehouse was rolled back. Inside, amid the rows of neat carcasses, a man in a chesterfield coat examined his nails.

I'll go to Casa Rosa, he decided. He had learned some Spanish in Barcelona, maybe it would get him some place with the bar girl.

Casa Rosa was full and cheerful for a late afternoon. He stowed his duffel behind the jukebox and found a slot at the bar.

"It's her day off," the bartender said. Yaaa! He felt the edge begin to slide from his mood and he ordered a double gin to try to recall it. Actually, the gin and his yearning for the girl were only symptomatic of what he really wanted, what he was postponing until he would be absolutely unable to prevent himself from doing it. He drank one gin after another, ameliorating them with tacos and cold beans from a bowl on the bar, his mind skimming over the Barrio skin joint in Barcelona with the girl astraddle his lap while he drank, over the open market in Tangier—three for the price of one, sailor—and the dark house in Athens. No, he would not permit that thought yet . . . first the Mediterranean from the deck of the *Falcon*, flat as blue marble, the sun blasting back from the sea, washing out the deck like an overexposed photo until his eyes felt full of sand.

"She was never off on Monday before," he said to the bartender.

"You're probably right." The bartender poured a free gin.

On board had been a kid from Amherst whose old man had a piece of the shipping company. He spent his days in the lee of the stack reading Byron and Durrell and Paul Bowles and had persuaded Steve to read some. (The Isles of Greece! What the hell did Byron know!) The gin warmed the memory and forced it to surface finally. The dark house in Athens with the boy brought in on a litter. Tell me, boy, what do you do when your father is at sea? The boy, no more than twelve, threw back his head and laughed, trailing his hand down the length of his bronze throat.

He was half drunk, but keenly drunk, with the edge recovered, capable of putting away another full bottle. Instead, he paid the bartender, left ten bucks for the missing bar girl, and went to the phone. It was in the back hall between the two johns, and the stink of pine-scented Lysol almost pitched his stomach, but he sat for a minute in the phone booth settling himself, warming the dime in his hand.

"Hello, Billy," he said into the phone. "It's Steve. Where are they?"

"In Brooklyn," came the voice. "Right off Jamaica Avenue."

■ ■ ■ ■

ELIZABETH ADDISON, KILLED IN A CRASH, *carted away* . . . The pull up the hill at 165th Street took so much of his breath, Ben could not complete the rhyme even in his mind. The rain began at his back, a cold rain for summer, chilling him, and instead of going into the subway, he went into the Medical Center and sat on a bench in the emergency room. Twice his mother had brought him here. He could not remember the reason, but once his head had been bleeding and he remembered the look on the young intern's face as he held the suture, ready to do his first bit of sewing on a human scalp. The second time, he had broken his arm falling over a skylight on the roof—or at least that was what his father had told him to say.

"You've got two left feet, Ben," his father said. "You

wouldn't last a minute aboard ship." Always in that patient voice, smooth as honey, smiling down at him.

"Why did you have to go and break your arm?"

Two cops came in, leading an old man clutching his chest. They put him into a high-backed wooden wheelchair and he sat with his head back, staring at the ceiling, his face as gray as the stone stanchion of the bridge. The resident finished a story he was telling to the nurse and they were laughing as he put his stethoscope in his ears and bent down to listen to the old man's dying heart.

From outside came the low moan of an ambulance siren. Ben moved by the door, where he could get a better look. The resident looked up briefly, his concentration on the old man interrupted by the possibility of something worse than what he was contending with. The litter bearers came at a gallop. They carried a crimson woman. Her hair, her face and arms were covered with blood. It had soaked the litter and was dripping to the floor as the bearers conferred with the nurse. As they stood there for that brief moment, the woman raised one thin bloody arm and moved it slowly back and forth as if she were administering last rites to herself. Ben felt his stomach churn but he could not turn away.

"What happened?" he said to the woman. She turned her head as if she had heard. Her mouth opened but no sound came.

"Are you her son?" said the nurse.

"What happened?" He could not stop saying this

ridiculous thing. Then they took her into a room and pulled the curtain.

He walked outside and threw up in the gutter and headed for the subway. There was no place else to go but home.

■　■　■　■

"DID YOU FIND HIM?" ROONEY ASKED.

"Find who?" Julie Williams was working a large piece of cuticle between her teeth and she had little patience for his questions.

"The Man," Rooney said. He hoped his voice sounded casual and unthreatening, but he was afraid there was an edge to it.

"You are such a stupid bastard," Julie said. "How did you get so stupid?"

Rooney sighed. He told himself that Julie did not actually mean this, that she said it only because she was angry and frustrated, and that what they were doing together was therapeutically sound, and that by ventilating her feelings and having them accepted, she would learn to trust. In his books he knew this to be true, but yet, in her presence, he did feel stupid, or perhaps helpless was a better word.

"Are you tired or something?" she said in response to

his sigh. "I'm not keeping you up, am I?" She jumped out of her chair and went to the window.

"No, you're not keeping me up." But he was weary. One day he must study this interview and see what went wrong. In the psychological journals they never sounded like this.

All he or anyone knew about this child was that she had been left in the Children's Shelter in the city one hot summer afternoon. She was seven then, thin and irritable, and for days she paced like an animal, refusing food, refusing to talk, squatting in any open space to urinate. Rooney had read the sparse history over and over as if he would find a clue to her past, about which she refused to speak. Julie could not or would not remember her mother's name or where they had lived, or anything, for that matter, about her life before she came to the School. It was as though the part of her brain which had contained those facts had dried up and blown away, for all the information she was able to recall. A face maybe, here and there; a lightbulb swinging from a ceiling; a man intervening. He wore a hat. Or did he? A moustache? It had been too dark to see.

"Do you think the Man is your father?" Rooney said.

"Jesus, Rooney," she said, "you never give up, do you?" She started for the door and he knew he must do something now to keep her from leaving.

"Maybe he was your friend," he said.

"Man, you are pathetic!" Julie said. She stomped out of the room, slamming the door behind her.

On the lawn, Odie stopped her. Since the riot, Julie had found a place among the important kids at the School, and people like Jim Dickenson, who was a firesetter, and Tao, who pitched a no-hitter against the local high school, and Odie, who could steal the badge off the chief of police, stopped her and passed the time of day and caught up on the news.

Odie spent his days and nights stealing. He could not resist. He stole from the five-and-ten, the parking meters, the phone boxes, from smaller boys and from larger girls, and while he was standing there talking to Julie, he stole a dollar from the hip pocket of her pants and then laughed and gave it back. He kept most of his loot in a hole he dug down near the railroad tracks. As he got older, he stole cars, jewelry, and the contents of cash registers. This Odie, at twelve, could leave the scene without a trace or a clue, could be in and out and gone and have whatever it was buried down by the tracks before anybody knew what hit them. The day before Thanksgiving, he stole six turkeys from the A & P and buried them in the ground, just for the hell of it.

"I got five bottles of Scotch," Odie was saying. "Chivas Regal. You come down to the hole tonight and we'll have a party."

"O.K.," Julie said. She was flattered, but her face showed nothing.

"Tell Mrs. Meredith to make us some sandwiches." Odie laughed, but Julie's face remained stony.

"I'll tell her," Julie said. Out of the corner of her eye she thought she saw the Man go into the gymnasium.

Odie followed her gaze.

"That was Ferguson who went into the gym," he said. They all knew of her preoccupation with the Man.

"Who says so?" Julie said. She ran off to see for herself.

■ ■ ■ ■

HE WAS SITTING AT THE KITCHEN TABLE, drinking gin and eating soda crackers, when they got home from the Botanical Gardens.

Winnie ran to him and he pulled her on his lap and she whispered into his ear.

"I told Billy Behrens that we were moving to Brooklyn," she said.

"That's my girl," Steve said, stroking her hair. "And who is Billy Behrens?"

"Her lover," Carol Ann said.

Steve looked at his older daughter over the top of his glass.

"Where did you learn that word?"

Carol Ann turned on the water in the sink. She was

always caught between wanting to please him and kill him and sometimes a little of both.

"I read it," she said. But there was too much acid in her voice and he bristled. He put Winnie down and strolled around the room, looking as if for the first time at his tall, twelve-year-old daughter.

"So you read," he said softly. "Is that a fact?" He walked slowly around and around the room, stalling, while he decided what to do with her. This child had never had much importance for him—never the importance of Ben, or Winnie, whom he liked despite himself, or even Ray, whom he considered a frail and harmless boy. Before this minute, Carol Ann had managed to cancel herself out with him, to move without disturbing the air about him, or to talk without his hearing. As for Philip, who was now sitting on the bed where he and Ray and Ben slept, his arms crossed, hugging himself, rocking back and forth, as for Philip, nothing.

"Where is Ben?" Steve said.

"What?" Carol Ann knew the heat was off her, and she felt the joy of the reprieved. "What did you say, Daddy?"

Steve refilled his glass and raised it slightly in a toast to her.

"Here's to you, lover," he said.

She blushed and turned back to the sink, confused by him—but at the same time—lover? that meant something else, like the two she had seen in Prospect Park, the girl with her dress up to her waist. Lover? She rinsed off the breakfast dishes, banging them on the drain, aware that he was still looking at her.

She glanced down at herself. "Oh, Jesus," she said aloud. The zipper of her blue jeans was open.

■　■　■　■

TELL ME NO STORY, TELL ME NO LIE, TELL ME *you love me, swear and hope to die.*

Sara hummed on her way to the subway. Friday, and that meant two days to catch up, to shop, to clean, to be with the kids, to look them over, to try to make up. Friday. The Brooklyn train roared into the station, and as the faces flashed past, she thought she saw Ben in a forward car. No, only a boy who looked like him. This boy, her favorite of all of them, this boy who set off her most complicated feelings and whom, because of this, she tried to ignore, to put out of her mind what was happening to him, this boy would be home with his brothers and sisters, looking after things. But she was sure it was Ben in the car, and as the train started out of the station, she made her way toward him.

He was in the front car, standing next to the motor-man's cubicle, watching the tracks through the front window as the train hurtled through the darkness. She watched him for a moment, his body swaying with the motion of the train. He was stocky, but with a graceful slope to his shoulders, the awkward grace of an athlete. He would be bigger than his father, and that thought, appearing suddenly in the hurtling train, caused her to tremble. She too was now in the tightening circle. That is why Ben is here, she thought, and she ran to him, bumping against the other passengers, as if the danger were here, now, on this train.

"Well, Ben, fancy meeting you here."

"We got separated." He tried to patch together a story to tell her, but the suddenness of her appearance had thrown him. She smiled.

"Where did you go today?"

"The Botanical Gardens." It slipped out, and he put out his hand, as if he could retract the words.

"I know you never stay home," she said. "I've known that for a long time."

"How did you know?" He looked relieved.

"Once I forgot something, and when I went back, there you were, heading for the subway. That day you went to the Planetarium."

"Carol Ann likes the Planetarium. We've been there five times."

She put her arm across his shoulders and together they watched the tracks curve out of sight into the darkness ahead of them.

"Your father will probably be home one of these

days," she said. She had never discussed Steve before with Ben, but somehow in the impersonal subway car, surrounded by the remnants of the rush hour, she could manage.

"I know it," Ben said. He felt a rush of questions in his throat, but he could ask none of them.

"This time, I'm sure he won't find us," she said.

"He always finds us."

"This time I made very sure that no one knew where we were going. Not even the post office."

"That's what you said last time." He had not meant to sound accusing, and although he was looking straight ahead, he could see her shoulders sag and feel her arm around him go lax.

"We could go to Lost Mountain, Wyoming," he said suddenly, as if to cheer her up.

"Where? That's silly."

"Lost Mountain. He could never find us."

"What on earth would we do in Lost Mountain?" she said.

"The same thing we do here. Only he wouldn't be there."

They rode in silence the rest of the way. When they came up the stairs into the street, both of them walked slowly until she said: "How would you like to stop off for a hamburger, just you and me."

He grinned. He had never had a meal with just his mother alone, without at least one other person. He grew suddenly shy, and as she spoke and as he looked at her, his shyness made him more acutely aware of her, as though he were a grown man in love.

They went into a White Tower and sat side by side at the counter. She let him order what he wanted without asking him if he were sure and without suggesting something else. He ordered two hamburgers and a chocolate drink. She ate nothing, but had coffee, and she turned halfway on her stool and watched him as he fiddled with the napkins and drummed on the counter with his thumbs.

"I never knew you were left-handed," he said, when the hamburgers arrived. She laughed. "I mean I watched you use your left hand, but I didn't think about it much." When she laughed, the tired lines left her face and she looked younger and very pretty. He was aware that he would remember her face like this, her head back as she laughed, the two of them sitting under the harsh light of the White Tower.

"You see," he said, as if he were taking up an unfinished conversation that both of them were eager to complete, "we figured that if we went places like the zoo and the museums, you couldn't get mad about that, but if we asked you, you might have said no."

"You are right," she said. "I might have."

"I wanted to go to the beach, but I was always outvoted."

"I'm glad of that," she said, looking down into her coffee. "You swim out too far." She said this more in praise than criticism, and he coughed to hide his pleasure. She wiped some catchup from his mouth, and he started to pull back as he would have at home, but somehow her doing it here in this White Tower restaurant was different and didn't make him feel like a baby. He stopped eating so fast, knowing that as soon as he was finished, she would want to go home.

"How does Philip manage?" she said. The laugh signs were gone now and her face clouded.

"Oh, he's O.K. You know, he's slow to go places with because he's always looking for junk. Yesterday he found a silver coin in the gutter. Ray said it was French. It was under something—a piece of green paper or some damned leaf or something."

He had never sworn in front of her before and their eyes met briefly and then slid away. She let it pass, and he knew that in that moment something had changed for them, only he could not decide whether it was for better or for worse. He would try to find out.

"He's a bastard," he said quietly.

Sara looked down at her hands and turned so that she faced the counter and away from him.

"I know it," she said, knowing that they were through talking about Philip and were back on Steve again.

Ben motioned to the waiter and ordered coffee, although he had never drunk it before. He knew now that the change was for the better but that it carried with it certain responsibilities which he must attend to as quickly as he could.

"You ought to quit that sonofabitch. I mean what the hell, what have you got to lose?"

His mother looked at him. Her eyes were as wide as a child's and for a moment he was afraid he had blown the whole thing and that she was going to cry and then what would he do? But she didn't cry. She kept looking at him and he saw more new things about her that he hadn't seen before: her hair was almost red and curled softly behind her ear; the wedding ring was gone from her left hand.

"Nothing to lose, I suppose."

When his coffee came, she poured milk and sugar in it as if she had always done it for him, as if she knew it was the only way he could gag it down.

"Well then!" he said, as if the matter were all settled; as if Steve had been miraculously erased from their lives.

"Well then," she said, musing, "well then, if it were as easy as that, I would have done it long ago. Long ago before he hurt you. And me. And all of us."

"What do you mean?" he said. He was conscious that his voice was rising and that he was in danger of losing all he had won.

"It's more complicated than it seems," she said, and

with this, her eyes stopped looking like those of a child and she was again his mother, protecting him from meanings that he was too young to comprehend, shutting him out of a part of her life that for a brief time she had been willing to share.

"Let's go home," she said. "The kids will be worried."

They walked side by side through the street, he with his hands in his pockets and his head bent, she humming a tune that he could only half hear.

■ ■ ■ ■

MADELINE HAD BEEN RAPED BY HER FATHER when she was seven years old, although rumor had it that she was younger. This was common knowledge at the School, the boys talking about how it would be physiologically possible. They speculated on various positions and devices the father must have used, exciting themselves with the talk. The girls said what a dirty man her father must have been, and that he should have been thrown in jail for life, or electrocuted. When Ben discovered this about Madeline, shortly after he and Ray had been left at the School, he had gone to her and stared, trying to see in her face any evidence remaining from the raping. He knew that this was rude and that it would embarrass Madeline, but he could not help himself. She hung her head, knowing his thoughts, until finally he said: "My father did the same thing to me."

"You're kidding!" she said. She stopped hanging her head and smiled, and after that, she began to take care of him.

Later, when they began going to their shack down by the tracks, she would tell him what happened, since she remembered every detail of her relationship to her father, or at least she thought she did. The truth was that she had had to tell the story of her father so many times for various authorities and for children who insisted on an account of it that she found the telling diminished rather than heightened her memory. So she made up her own story for Ben out of what might have been. In this way, she could recapture a portion of her pride.

"We lived in a big house," she would begin, settling down on their little bed and pulling Ben down beside her, "with tall trees and a wide lawn."

"How wide?" Sometimes Ben could not resist teasing her.

"The lawn went on as far as you could see." She found that if she stroked the back of his neck while she was recounting her story, he would interrupt less and that his questions came just frequently enough to convince her that he had not fallen asleep.

"The house had three stories and I had the entire third floor to myself. A regular suite, I had, and a maid, whose only responsibility was to tend to my wishes." At times like this, Madeline's language became extremely flowery. When she finally got around to introducing the other characters who inhabited this baronial manor, they were saints or great beauties or people of such undisputable character that Ben could not even laugh; instead, he nuzzled his face against her big warm body and listened to the slow, sure sound of her heart. This sound, this cadence, this particular pitch, he was to remember for a long time, and he would have been able, should the need have arisen, to differentiate it from a hundred other heartbeats.

When Madeline got to describing her father's face, Ben would rouse himself for more acute listening, knowing that the raping scene was not far off, and that the long wait, through the gardens and rooms and costumes of the characters, was worth it.

"My father had a gentle face," Madeline would say. "Despite the fact that he wore glasses."

Sometimes the train would come by as Madeline was telling her story, and the cardboard walls of their little shack would tremble against the vibration of the train, but Madeline would keep talking as though, if she once stopped, everything would evaporate from her mind. If the train came by during the good parts of the story, then Ben would have to put his ear next to her mouth, since the roar was so loud it obliterated everything.

On the way back to the School from these outings,

Madeline was quiet and she would hold Ben's hand. It was then that she would think about what really happened: her father half drunk and threatening, the tiny apartment littered with bottles and his filthy underwear.

■ ■ ■ ■

THEY CLIMBED THE STAIRS, BEN LEADING the way, since some of the bulbs lighting the halls had been smashed and never replaced. At the next-to-last landing, Ben turned to his mother.

"I don't hear Mr. and Mrs. Ruiz fighting," he said. He did not particularly care about the Ruizes at the moment, but it was a stall against going on. Sara sensed this and leaned against the wall.

"Maybe they went to the movies," she said.

"We could go to the movies," Ben said quickly. "There's a good one at the RKO."

Sara shook her head. "We can't do that, Ben."

"But why?" He felt his voice rising again, and suddenly there were tears in his eyes. Was the bulb dim enough so that she wouldn't see? "We never do anything but go to the goddamned Planetarium."

She came to him, but he pulled away, turning his head.

"Come on now. Let's go in and make some popcorn," she said.

"No," she shouted. "No, he's in there!"

"What? Did you see him?"

"He's there all right."

"You're a silly thing," she said, putting her arm around him.

But as they approached the apartment door, it opened before them, and there he was, holding his gin glass and smiling.

■ ■ ■ ■

MRS. RUIZ WAS LEANING ON HER ELBOWS ON the fifth-floor window of her apartment when Sara and Ben passed on the sidewalk below. She was dreaming of home—Santurce—and trying to figure if she could save the air fare by Christmas. This time she would stay there and never come back to this rotten man she married. She would get a job at the university where it was cool and beautiful or at the Medical School in old San Juan where the professors spoke in whispers and wore long white coats.

She watched the woman and the boy turn into the building and she sighed. This young woman knew a kind of terror that she herself had never known, despite the fact that her husband was a rotten, lazy, whoring bastard.

"Luisa." His voice behind her was as soft as a young boy's. "Luisa, come to bed. You must not sit there in the rain."

"And why not?" she said, trying to make her voice sound gruff.

"Because you will get a cold and then pneumonia and then die and I would grieve for a thousand days and a thousand nights."

"And what would you do on the thousandth and first night?" she said. But she turned away from the window.

■ ■ ■ ■

THE RAIN BEAT AGAINST THE SKYLIGHT IN the hall. They stood unmoving for a moment, Steve catching his wife's gaze and holding it. He thought she looked pale and wondered if it was because he had surprised her or if she was ill. Behind him stood Winnie and Carol Ann and Ray, their shoulders touching, as if they formed some foolish, unarmed rear guard.

"Come in," he was saying, curving his arm and bowing from the waist. "You see before you the loyal troops of Ali Koranah, trembling with joy at the arrival of their master. Come, come, come," he said, taking Ben by the elbow. "Don't let this palace frighten you away."

From the background, Winnie began to giggle.

"Oh, Daddy," she said, "you're funny. This isn't a palace."

"Of course it's a palace," he said, swinging into the mood. "The Palace of Solomon, and here before you stands the Queen of Sheba herself, although I must admit I didn't know until this moment that the Queen of Sheba was a redhead."

With this, Carol Ann and Ray sat down at the table as if they were watching a show. Ben went into the bedroom as quietly as he could and closed the door. He could still hear his father's voice, caught up in the storytelling, and he heard the others laugh, sometimes even his mother.

On the far corner of the bed, Philip still rocked back and forth, the light from the street casting his davening shadow on the wall.

"Come over here," Ben said. "Nobody's going to hurt you." Ben was aware that he sounded like his mother, but the little boy did not look up from his endless preoccupation. Ben sat on the window ledge and looked into the rain-swept street. He tried to shift his mind to some other time, some other place, to quiet his trembling, but the sounds of laughter from the kitchen and the Spanish radio station playing from the Ruizes' bedroom kept drawing him back into the room, into the last circle of his terror. He knew that in a moment his father would open the door.

"Hello, Ben."

Steve stood there, his head tilted to one side, a curious, listening expression on his face.

"Do you want to join us?"

"No," Ben said.

"Your father home from the sea, telling everyone of his adventures in exotic lands?" He sat down on the bed and his manner changed, as if he were with a buddy, a shipmate.

"I'm going to take you with me some day, Ben," he said, "let you see beyond the scope of your nose. Bright boy like you should ride something beside the BMT, I mean God almighty, if you keep this up, you'll end in that graveyard with the rest of the Polacks. Ben, Ben." He reached out and grabbed the boy's shoulder, as if to cajole him, as he would his buddy who had spent too long in the bar. Ben pulled away—imperceptibly—but Steve felt it and he took another drink from his glass as if to prepare himself for another mood which was about to descend.

"What is this?" he said, jerking a thumb toward Philip.

"Why, that's Philip." Off-guard, Ben's voice was guileless. "He's my brother."

"Well now, is that a fact?" The old honey back in his voice. "Philip. Did I give you a name like that?" Steve took Philip's head in his hands. The boy's translucent eyes showed no sign—it was as if the man did not exist. Steve, looking into those vacant eyes, hesitated, out of his range. He hung there for a second, and Ben, noting this, thought run, run, get out now, let him work on Philip for a change. Steve cocked his head as if he had heard the thought and the interference broke the spell.

"Well, Philip," he said, "let's take a look at you."

■　■　■　■

THAT DAY, THAT SUMMER DAY WITH THE thermometer over 102, the concentration of sulphur dioxide turned the sky yellow and held the air unmoving and unbreathable under the weight of the heat, trapping the city in its yellow envelope. The Man had gone, had left the apartment before there was any light in the sky. In the living room he paused for a moment, looked at the sleeping forms of the two little boys on the couch. The third slept on a blanket on the fire escape. From the bedroom he could hear Bernice snoring, her heavy arm over the shoulder of the little girl. He found his cigarettes on the coffee table, rummaged for matches, and not finding them, put on the naked bulb for a second over his head. Someone in the bedroom stirred, and he strained to see through the darkness. He saw, or he thought he saw, the little girl lift her head, the faint light of the street catching her dark eyes looking at him. Then he ran down the four flights of the gutted staircase, the rotting boards groaning under his feet.

He had done what he could. He had given Bernice money every payday, telling her to buy the groceries and pay the rent first, but in three days she would have blown it all and then he would have to borrow more from his friends to get them through the week. He tried lugging in the food himself and buying clothes for the children, but she would not speak to him then, sitting for hours in a chair by the window drinking from a bottle she got God knows where, or flying into fits of rage anywhere: on the street, in the schoolyard. The police knew her, and if they did not bring her home, the street children would form a circle around her, taunting, shouting abuse, jumping back from the angry thrusts of her fists as if they were young toreros. Olé, fat cow!

In the street he looked back up at the window. Was the child's face there? He could not tell. But he raised his hat anyway, like a country gentleman, to wish her goodbye.

When Bernice awoke to find him gone, her instinct told her that she would not see him again, that she had pushed him too far. Although this bothered her deeply, she was unable to react to it, and instead she lay there, thinking about the heat and wondering if it would rain. All over town, she thought, people lying on the bed thinking if it's going to rain. She wondered how many were for, and how many against.

By ten, the temperature had reached ninety-two. Bernice could see from her bed that the boy on the fire escape had gone, and that meant she would not see him until late that night when he would show up looking for food. Already he was a stranger, running with his own pack, looking at her with angry eyes. The other two would not be long to follow him.

"We got to go to the Welfare," she said, swinging her legs over the side of the bed. "You hear me?"

"Yes." The little girl was sitting cross-legged, looking at her toes. "He's gone," she said in a whisper.

"You shut up about that," Bernice said. "When we get down there, you just shut up and let me do the talking." It was her rage that got Bernice up and moving; otherwise, she might have stayed longer in the bed, pretending he was only making the coffee, pretending that he would come in any minute and tell her to get her sweet ass over and let him in.

"Just one word out of you," she said, grabbing the little girl's arm and shaking her, "and you'll be sorry you ever learned to talk!"

She pushed the child away from her, and the little girl began to cry.

"And shut up with that crying. I'm nervous enough as it is." As she set the water on to boil for coffee, the truth of the matter rushed in: everything gone . . . the man, the boys, the money. There wasn't even enough coffee to make a full pot.

The little girl dried her face on the pillow and put on her blue jeans and sandals. She was looking for her blouse when she saw an old shirt of his balled up in the corner of the closet. He must have forgotten it, she thought, and she held it close to her face, smelling his strong scent in the fabric. She smoothed the shirt out over her knee. It had been a light blue Oxford cloth, but now it was faded nearly white, the collar frayed almost away. She put her arms in the sleeves and pulled it over her thin shoulders. It hung below her knees, but she rolled up the sleeves and buttoned it up anyway. Then she went to the kitchen, where her mother stood next to the stove.

"I'm going down," she said.

"You're not going anywhere except with me," Bernice said.

"Yes, I am."

The little girl's voice was almost a whisper, but Bernice heard in it a streak of stubbornness which made her rankle.

"You are going with *me*," she said, whirling around to see the little girl standing there in the man's shirt. "Where the hell did you get that?"

She reached out to take the shirt off the child, but the child jumped back and the shirt ripped down the front. With this, the child ran out of the apartment and down the stairs, leaving the woman standing there puzzled and angry.

By this time, it was 94 degrees and the asphalt on the street was going soft with the heat and people went about their business slowly as if to save themselves for what was coming in the afternoon. The child, however, ran down the block, darting in and out of the produce and the milk and bread that was being unloaded for the stores, and in and out of the slow-moving people until she came to Eighth Avenue, where, still running, she turned south, and, still running, arrived at Woolworth's five blocks later. Here she stopped to compose herself and to decide what color thread—white or blue—she needed. Then she went in and was out again in under a minute, out before the salesgirls could see what it was she had stolen, out and running for the park. She spent the rest of the day, as the thermometer rose to 102 at four that afternoon, sitting with her back against a tree, sewing up the tear in the shirt. She had never done work of this type before, so the first three or four attempts were ragged and not what she had in mind and she had to rip them out. Finally she was satisfied that the tear was mended as well as could be expected, and she started home.

When she got there, her mother was drunk and sitting in her chair by the window, singing *Nobody Loves You When You're Down and Out*, and when she saw the little girl she said: "Now don't you agree with that, Julie Williams? Don't you just have to admit it's the truth?"

■　■　■　■

MR. FERGUSON WATCHED THE NEW COT-
tage parents arrive in their brand-new, blue-vinyl-topped
Grand Prix. The man got out and stretched himself in a
slow lazy way and walked around the car, inspecting it
for dust, while his wife went into the administration
building. Mr. Rose had told the staff that they were
coming: Dave and Wilma from Albuquerque, New
Mexico. Fine young couple, Mr. Rose had said.

Dave removed a soft white cloth from the trunk of the
car and began to polish the hood and Mr. Ferguson knew
from watching him this short a time that he was bad
news. Too good-looking, Mr. Ferguson thought, and too
lazy, letting his wife attend to the business. He had seen
this type come and go through the years, following the
trail of children's institutions across the country, staying
until there was trouble or until boredom drove them to
the next place. Well, it would be something to tell his
wife: that, despite their fancy car, the woman had runs in
her stockings.

Mr. Ferguson went through the gymnasium to a
pachysandra bed he had planted the week before which
needed watering. He bent down to test the soil and to
remove a few weeds, when Julie came running out. She
stopped and danced around him.

"Did you see a man come out that door?" she said.

"Just me," Mr. Ferguson said.

"Not you," she said. "A man!"

Mr. Ferguson had to laugh. This kid was always running, running like she was being chased by a band of lunatics.

"Shit," Julie said, "you're no help."

And with that, she ran off, straight through the pachysandra and across the lawn.

■ ■ ■ ■

THE MOVES OF THE GAME WERE RUNNING out and Ben thought: if you don't get out now, in this split second, this is the way you're going to die: not by being hit by a truck, or smashed in the head by a derrick, or drowning, as Sara thought, or struck by lightning—the things he had imagined and had prepared himself to endure—but by a small man in a navy turtleneck sweater, a small, reasonable man who was smiling at his brother in the dark room. Run! But there he was awake in the dream, his feet glued to the floor, ass-deep in the cement of his indecision. Then Philip looked up at him, eyes as pale as water, no demands in his expression, just a blank look as though Ben were a part of the wall, as though the glance might be through a window—the idle charting of a bird's flight. Philip, as usual, was leaving it all up to him.

"Stay away from him," Ben said.

His father laughed.

"You are a funny little boy," he said to Ben, "trying to be a man." He took a step closer and struck Ben in the face.

In the past when this had happened, when the blows came, Ben knew that if he could survive the first, he could survive the rest. He would turn off his mind and listen to such things as the sound the blows made on the inside of his head, or the increased racing of his heart, or sometimes, if he could, he would look for a fly or a roach on the wall and watch its progress, giving it a life, a name, a past, and making up a present for it as he was being beaten.

But this time Ben did not turn off his mind. Instead, he wheeled and picked up the lamp that stood on the table next to the bed. The cord ripped from the wall, shredding, sending a ray of sparks across the floor. In one motion, he swung the lamp and crashed it against the side of his father's head, knocking Steve to the floor. The little man sat there looking as though he were deep in thought as the blood ran down his cheek.

And Philip sat and rocked and would not get off the bed even though Ben yelled at him to run and get their mother.

■ ■ ■ ■

IN THE NEXT APARTMENT, THE RADIO
went quiet as Mrs. Ruiz put her ear to the wall.

"The husband must be home," she said to Mr. Ruiz.

■ ■ ■ ■

WHEN STEVE RECOVERED, HE WIPED AWAY
the blood in a slow, fastidious way as if he were preparing to enter an elegant restaurant. Ben had never
struck him before, and when he finished tending himself,
Steve looked at the boy with a new interest.

Ben put himself between his father and Philip, trying
to edge the little boy off the bed and toward the door.
This pitiful defense amused Steve and he allowed Ben
to struggle for a moment with the unwilling child who
could not give up his preoccupation.

"He doesn't seem to listen to you," Steve said. "Maybe
you're losing your influence around here after all." Ben
turned and stared.

Hang the monkey in the tree. Something in the boy's
face brought this singsong phrase to Steve's mind, and
in the silence that engulfed them, with Ben standing
trembling to protect the little boy who rocked and

rocked on the bed, while he held Ben's eyes in the sharp grip of his own, keeping him from moving in that way, Steve saw himself at the mercy of his own two brothers, swinging upside down in a tree where they had tied him. With his pants off.

The rain came in a torrent now and over the bed a leak had sprung, the drops falling on Philip, wetting his thin hair and running into his eyes. The rain hit flat on the tar roof over their heads and rattled in the tin gutters, overflowing them and setting the windows awash, melting the streetlights and the forms of the people racing for cover into a swirl of wet red and yellow. And dark purple.

Hang the monkey in the tree. They tied a pine cone on him and made a joke about the pinus cone.

"Your little brother is getting wet," Steve said. "What kind of a keeper are you to let a thing like that happen?"

His voice was so soft that Ben could barely hear him: always a danger signal. In the street, a garbage can was tumbled over by the wind and rolled down the sidewalk. That and the rain were the only sounds. It was as if all the people and all the traffic had been rerouted. Only the people in this apartment had been allowed to stay. But for what reason? Ben yearned to look into the street for a clue. Maybe there was a flood and it was already too late. Maybe the tide was rising all the way from Jamaica Bay to save him, lapping over the hoods of the cars, floating away the groceries from the shelves of Finast

Foods, creeping up the sides of Elizabeth Addison's grave.

If he had had an ax, he could not have unlocked himself from his father's stare. But because of Philip, he seemed less paralyzed than usual, and he took a cautious step backward, toward the bed, where he might get a better grip on the boy and pull him to safety.

"After all," Steve was saying, "a little maggot like him needs all the help he can get. Although why the hell you bother beats me. He's got so many screws loose, you could put him on an assembly line for a month and he'd never get tightened up."

Ben reached behind him and grabbed Philip by the shirt, making a ball of the fabric in his hand so that Philip was as close to him as possible. He must keep his father talking and distracted for a second and then in one motion—

"There's nothing wrong with Philip," Ben said.

Steve leaned back on his heels and laughed, the mashed colors from the street playing on his face through the rain-swept window.

"Do you know what they do with little freaks like him in Java?" Steve asked.

"No." Ben tightened his grip on the little boy's shirt. A signal. He would have to open the door with his left hand and push Philip through.

"They slit them right up the middle and feed them to the crows."

Now! Ben jumped, dragging Philip behind him, and reached for the door. But in less effort than it would take a young cat, Steve was there before him, blocking the way.

"Don't try to outwit your old man," Steve said.

He reached over Ben's shoulder and picked up Philip as if he were a rag and twirled him around and around over his head. The little boy covered his ears and began to moan.

The sight of Philip, or perhaps the sound he was making, triggered in Ben a kind of fury he had not known before. He lunged for his father's throat, missed the first time and lunged again as the little man sidestepped like a flamenco dancer, sending Ben crashing into the door. Then Ben kicked his father in the groin with his hard, schoolboy shoes and Steve screamed and held his injured parts. Philip somehow landed on his feet, and Ben shoved him out the door, sending him sprawling into the kitchen. For a second Ben saw his mother and Carol Ann and Winnie sitting at the kitchen table. Ray was pouring coffee and he and all of them froze—their hands froze in mid-air and their expressions all froze on their faces. They looked like dummies in a store window, nailed into place.

There was no contest with his father after that. Although Ben fought and clawed and tried to get under the bed to escape the blows, Steve had lost control and his fury filled the room. At last Ben fell unconscious over the bed with a broken arm and with internal injuries which caused him to bleed from the mouth.

It was Mrs. Ruiz who called the police, finally.

■ ■ ■ ■

"OH, LORD GOD," SAID BERNICE. THE LINE at the Welfare Center was halfway down the block and the doors hadn't opened yet. It was Friday and the temperature was 93 degrees at a quarter to nine. And she had a head like a tin can full of rocks. She did not know if she could make it to the door.

I'm going to make up something, she thought, something long and good that will take an hour or two to think about, and if I put my mind to that, maybe I'll get there. So she thought about Sam. Sweet Sam, long since departed yesterday, how would they make it without him? They went fishing once, took a taxicab to the Dyckman Street pier. He made Boston baked-bean sandwiches, but they didn't catch a damned fish. It didn't matter. Coming in with the coffee: get your sweet ass over . . . Wonder if he went to California? But she could not hold even Sam in her mind for more than a few minutes. Even after they opened the doors, the line didn't move. A woman began to scream at the guard, who folded his arms across his chest like a sentry. He had heard it before.

Bernice had brought Julie and the little boys—the big boy had not come home the night before—but the little boys grew restless and their play took them farther and farther down the block until they were gone from sight. The temperature was climbing. Her headache, which had been bad enough at home, was getting worse, throbbing behind her eyeballs and blurring her vision. The heat. Her stomach churned once and she thought she would go down, but she steadied herself on the child's shoulder.

"Go get your mama a soda from the corner," she said.

"I got no money," Julie said.

"Neither have I," Bernice said. "Go!"

Behind her, an old man sniggered. "Get me one too," he said.

But Julie had already gone.

Oh, for a cold drink of water, a tall glass with ice cubes in it, and then another one, just like the first. And an aspirin.

"I was here yesterday," the old man said.

Bernice did not like casual conversations in the street. The times when she was drunk in the street and was taunted or herded home, she put out of her mind. Even the fragments that remained she did not admit belonged to her—part of a picture show she had watched on TV.

"Yesterday I got inside," the old man said. Pride, as

though he had done something. "Right up to the counter."

Bernice did not even turn around.

"Then they closed for the day," he said.

Bernice finally looked at him. "You got an aspirin?" she said.

The old man laughed. "Me?" He blew his nose between his thumb and finger as if to emphasize the negative.

"I said to the man, 'How about taking just one more?' You know what he said?"

"Well then, have you got a cigarette?" Bernice said.

The old man shook his head. "He said to me, 'Who the hell do you think you are?'" He laughed as if that were a good joke.

"I would have split him in half," Bernice said.

"He didn't even look at me when he said it. Can you imagine that?"

"It don't take much to imagine that," Bernice said.

"I started to tell him who I was, since he didn't know," the old man continued. "I said, 'My name is James Melvin Garvey, I am seventy-four and I live on St. Nicholas Avenue.' I would have told him the rest of me, but he called the guard."

Bernice snorted. She was only half listening, thinking about her enormous thirst, but she was beginning not to mind the conversation.

"One day I am going to set that guard on fire," he said.

Bernice had to laugh. "I'll loan you the gasoline," she said.

■ ■ ■ ■

A BIG OVERHEAD FAN BLEW THE FLIES around in the candy store. When the door opened, it rattled a tiny bell and the woman who owned the place glanced up from her paper, over her glasses, over the narrow marble counter toward the door and the child. She was a fat woman who ate up most of her profits. She could read the paper with one eye and watch for shoplifters with the other. She had a voice like an old dog's bark.

"What you want?" she said.

"Nothing," Julie said.

"Then get out of here," said the woman.

"What kind of soda you got?" Julie said.

"What kind you want? You name it, I'll see if I got it." A sixty-five-year-old woman was robbed and murdered in the project elevator, according to the newspaper. By the time she got to the twelfth floor, they had slit her throat and taken her purse.

"A goddamned jungle," the woman said.

"Strawberry," Julie said.

The woman lowered her eyes to check on strawberry and Julie slipped a pack of bubble gum from the tray.

"No strawberry," said the woman.

Julie turned and walked from the store, setting the bell to jingling.

"Thieves and murderers," the woman said.

In the street, Julie tried to figure the best place to steal the soda. The A & P had a manager like a police dog, and the deli kept all the soda locked in the back, including the empties. The best place was probably off a delivery truck, and as she stood there thinking about this, feeling the heat closing in around her, a bus went by and she saw the Man sitting in it by the window. He was wearing an Oxford cloth shirt with the sleeves rolled halfway up, the way he always did. As he passed, she was sure that he glanced up and tipped his hat to her.

The bus was going at a good speed, hissing over the melted tar, honked ahead even faster by a delivery truck behind it. Julie set off at a run to try to catch sight of the Man again. Two blocks away, the bus pulled in toward the curb long enough to let off a young boy, and then it sped off again, leaving a trail of black, acrid smoke. Julie ran for sixteen blocks, once getting as far as the door, but the driver had his mind on other things and did not hear her knocking there. She never got close again, and finally she tripped and sprawled exhausted in front of a funeral parlor, where she lay until she caught her breath.

It occurred to her as she lay gasping that her mother was still standing on the welfare line and would beat the hell out of her if she didn't go back. She would probably beat the hell out of her anyway for taking so long to bring the soda.

■　■　■　■

THE LIGHT FROM THE KITCHEN BULB SHONE on Sara's hair. She had called them to sit at the table, and something in her voice made them wary. Their father was away, this time in the Pacific, but he would be home soon, she said, and now they must talk of certain things.

Then she paused, and with the side of her thumbnail she made a tracing on the tabletop, her thoughts suddenly departed from them, flying back over time to that first afternoon she had known him. It was a cold fall day, with the leaves blowing down. He had found a bunch of flowers—amber chrysanthemums—left discarded on the grass, and had presented them to her like a child, smiling and holding the bouquet at a stiff arm's length.

She straightened herself and began again, as if she were chairing a meeting, her hands on the table in front of her like gavels.

"As you know," she said, her voice too loud and unfamiliar, "your father is a difficult man . . ."

She had never seen Steve smile with such openness and candor again, and yet that was what she held in her memory when she tried to cope with his cruelty to Ben. "You exaggerate, love, you exaggerate," he would say. "Ask the boy, if you don't believe me." He would smile at her and ruffle her hair, but the smile looked dead on his lips. Then he would hold her, and when she could not see his face, she would search her mind for the time when none of this had happened.

Ben watched her, not listening. He watched her mouth and he thought: you have the same teeth in your mouth day after day, year after year—what a pain in the ass. He noticed a tiny gold filling close to the gum line. The sight was so intimate, he turned away.

She stopped speaking and looked at him. Winnie was gathering her breath to cry. He had heard nothing, and suddenly he was furious at Sara. Why hadn't she spoken louder so that he could hear. Carol Ann was saying, Oh dammit to hell, over and over again. Philip slid down in his chair until he disappeared under the table, where he lay with his arms around Ben's leg. And Ray, big shit, was trying to keep from crying by biting the corner of his lip until it bled.

Ben got up from the table, having heard nothing, and after he loosened Philip's grip, he walked out of the apartment. In the hallway he could hear Mrs. Ruiz yelling—or was she singing?—against a background of Mr.

Ruiz's persistent basso and the Spanish music station. In the street, he passed the deli, which was still open and empty, and turned north toward the cemetery.

The street was littered with garbage and tin cans and two exquisitely wrecked automobiles, their hoods and trunks sprung, their upholstery shredded, every glass and fiber set upon as if it were a pestilence to be destroyed. On the back seat of one of the cars lay a bright red crayon, brand new and shining under the street lamp, and the sight of this somehow pierced the barrier of his mind, letting through a whisper of what his mother had said: "You and Ray." But just the words. No meaning.

He scaled the cemetery fence. Black as pitch, now, since the light from the street was behind him. Only the stones led him down a familiar path: Edward Finney and the McMurtrys, white marble sentries marking his way to the old woman.

"God damn you, Elizabeth Addison!" he shouted, doing a dance like a crazy Indian on her grave. "God damn you, God damn you!" And with this, the gates of his mind fell back and his mother's words broke like eggs over his head, soaking his mind.

"I'm sending you and Ray to live in a nice school up on the Hudson River. Only for a little while until your father and I get things worked out."

Then he wept, his arms around Elizabeth Addison's headstone.

■ ■ ■ ■

FOR THREE DAYS, BERNICE SAT BY THE WIN-
dow staring. When the little boys came home, she made
no attempt to feed them, so they helped themselves to the
precious little in the refrigerator—a wizened apple, some
cream cheese brown at the edges, a box of cold cereal.
Then they went out to the park, and when it grew dark,
remembering the state Bernice was in, they slept under
a footbridge by the rowing lake. It was cooler there,
anyway, and they could look out at the stars.

Julie came later, afraid of Bernice's temper, and hoping
that enough time would have passed for her to forget
about the soda. When she saw her mother sitting by the
window, she sighed and knew that this was going to be
worse. She guessed that the boys must have come and
gone, but she herself was afraid to stay out all night. She
had heard too many stories, most of them true.

She found a box of rice in the cupboard, and although
she had never cooked rice before, it turned out fairly
well, despite the fact that it was slightly burned. She
offered a plate of it to her mother, but Bernice swept
away the dish as if it were a vision, spewing the rice onto
the floor. The child salvaged what she could and then
went to bed, lying there shivering, although the temperature, all that night, did not drop below 90 degrees.

At the window, Bernice sat without benefit of gin or

sense of time, or food. She was not aware that the boys had come and gone or that Julie had tried to feed her, or that there was any specific form or sequence to her life. What sounds she heard were sporadic and distorted, bent out of their usual shape by her unlistening mind.

At the Welfare Center she had been given a form to fill out and was told to come back with rent receipts and the children's birth certificates. She had walked back through the heat and up the five flights with such a bad headache that lights danced in front of her eyes. In the dark hallway of her building, she became totally blinded for a few minutes and was forced to rest there, leaning against the wall, until her vision cleared. She found a receipt from three months before, but nothing current. The birth certificates had long ago been misplaced, but she looked for them anyway, thinking she might discover them by accident. But in the sparse apartment there were no hiding places: no boxes with old letters and souvenirs, no drawers with surprises from the past. There was one closet in which hung the dress she was not wearing and the boys' winter jackets. At the moment the children had no underwear, no socks, no extra things of any kind. In the kitchen, only roaches filled the nooks and crannies.

The clerk rejected her application without looking up, without once meeting her eye, singsonging the denial from behind the desk as though he were reading from a paper. And finally, when she did not reply or move away, he looked up and said, "Habla español, is that it?"

He picked up a stack of applications and riffled through them. For a moment Bernice thought that this had something to do with her, that perhaps he was going to rescind the rule by finding a magic regulation among his papers. He was not a bad-looking man, she thought, with a silky moustache and small hands. She would try to rely on him. So she took a seat on the bench, not wanting to appear to hurry him or put him under any kind of pressure. Anyway, it was cooler here than in the street, although the smell was bad, although there were no windows open and no air except what came in as the doors were opened and closed.

Bernice sat down on the bench at one o'clock, her mind nowhere in particular except at first on the clerk, then touching here and there, without sequence, on a face, the particular style, the way the man who had left her had about him, rinsing his own socks every night; the look on her brother William's face the night he smashed up the car; the older boy gone too now—but drawing no conclusions from all of this; instead, closing her eyes against the glare and listening to the colors as they crossed her mind, imagining that the air was sweet again.

The woman beside her had three young children, their mouths stained with the chocolate she had brought to pacify them. One of them crawled into Bernice's lap, and she held him, automatically, unaware that he was there. The child's mother had been talking to her for an hour.

"I'll tell you one thing about the Old South. Those

side porches with that damn honeysuckle are rotten and busted . . ."

Bernice was singing to herself: *I'm going to get you, Adam Bagly, going to get you for my own.* Except she sang without tune, without sound, only the colors in her mind making the music.

". . . and some snot-nosed teen-aged kid is playing an electric guitar until all hours of the night. That sweet humming in the twilight is gone. Gone!" said the woman. Then the woman herself was gone and it was five o'clock and the applications clerk put on his wilted seersucker jacket and went home. Only a drunk remained, sleeping against a wall. The guard looked at his watch, tried to rouse the drunk, and when that failed, picked him up like a sack and set him down on the pavement outside. He came back puffing and stood in front of Bernice.

"We're closing, lady," he said.

Bernice did not hear him. She was sitting erect with her hands folded neatly in her lap, gazing at the chair where the clerk had been sitting, but not seeing it; instead, she was contemplating a lavender sea breaking against a coast of black rock.

The guard finally took her by the elbow and set her moving in the street. She began to walk, stepping as precisely as a dancer over the dog dung and around the garbage cans, crossing the street with the greatest finesse, inches to spare between a truck and taxi, brushing the side of a speeding station wagon. "Christalmighty!" the driver screamed. She climbed the stairs and sat down by the window, with no remembrance of the Welfare Center, or Sam the Man who had gone away. The lavender sea in her mind changed to green for a few hours, but that was the only thing that she was aware of.

■ ■ ■ ■

WILMA OPENED THE LAST SUITCASE, THIS one full of Dave's sweaters. Collecting them was a passion with him—all colors and designs, all cut to show the slope of his athlete's shoulders to best advantage. He preferred cashmeres and would often pay as much as eighty dollars for one, spending his last cent like a gambler, addicted as he was to his own vanity. He preferred to arrange them in the drawer himself when they settled in a new place, so she left the suitcase open on the bureau.

Wilma sighed and sat in the chair. They had come from a school for disturbed asthmatic children in the desert near Albuquerque where they had worked for seven months—she in the kitchen and he in charge of the recreation program. She had not minded it there, even the terrible heat of the summer had not bothered her, or the wheezing, mistrustful children who ate little and played less. The two serious librarian types who ran the place had not been much different from others they had

worked for, steeped in their endless psychological inter-
pretations of the children's every act and gesture. She
and Dave had learned enough of the jargon to pass, so to
speak, in a succession of these institutions, a handy knack
which kept them employed until the going got rough, as
it always did, when Dave lost control.

They had left Albuquerque two weeks before, without giving notice, without getting their last pay. Wilma
had not pressed him for the reason. She had seen the
crisis begin those last days of August, had watched the
lady directors set up a surveillance of Dave's activities:
the old familiar pattern. She knew it would not be long
and she wondered which child had been involved. She
considered staying behind, if they would have her, but in
the end she packed the bags as usual and got into the car
beside him.

"Where to?" he had said, as unmindful as a child.

"East," she said. If they were west, they went east. If
they were south, they went north. They would drive
until they found a likely place and then look for a
children's institution. Or, if they were running low on
cash, they would head for the nearest big city. They
banked on the fact that help was always hard to find in
such places—especially a nice, good-looking couple like
themselves who seemed to understand children so well.

After a while, Dave put on the car radio and Wilma
began to hum along with a country rock group that was
singing about true love.

■ ■ ■ ■

MADELINE WATCHED HIM FROM THE STEPS of Reese Cottage. He was wearing a light yellow cashmere sweater and cream-colored slacks and he walked with the pigeon-toed grace of an athlete. Fat cat, she thought, noticing the slope of his shoulders. Even from that distance, he was beautiful, and she narrowed her eyes over the top of her movie magazine and watched him polish the hood of his car. Then she saw Mr. Rose come out of the building with the woman and shake hands with him and go off with them, arms linked, toward Beakman, where the boys lived. The new houseparents.

After that, Madeline could not reinvolve herself in the story she had been reading about Candice Bergen (whom she hoped to look like some day, after she went on a diet). Instead, she ambled slowly across the lawn as though she might be going to the chapel, kicking aimlessly at the first few fallen leaves of the fall. When she got to the chapel, she ran quickly around to the back, scrambled up a bank, and hid herself behind a hedge. She knew she would have to wait awhile, so she read a bit more about Candice, about how she was a "now" person interested in causes and was thought to be, in some circles, an intellectual. Madeline made a mental note to read some of the classics before the year was out.

In about twenty minutes, Dave and Wilma walked

into the suite of rooms that was to be their quarters in Beakman. The woman unpacked a few things, and then she slumped down in a chair and kicked off her shoes. But the man seemed restless. He examined all the closets and the bureaus and tested the two neat twin beds, saying something to the woman that made her laugh. He took off his beautiful cashmere sweater and the shirt under it and stood at the window, as though he sensed someone might be watching, and rubbed his hands reflectively over the smooth brown muscles of his chest. Then he massaged the back of his neck, exposing his virile armpits and the long plane of his belly. Finally he turned back into the room and sprawled across the bed. Madeline sat watching them for another hour, although neither the man nor his wife moved.

■ ■ ■ ■

THEY WENT BY TRAIN.
Winnie was convinced they were going on a picnic and she packed all her picnic paraphernalia, including a doll and a bucket and spoon to dig with, in a string bag, which she dragged along behind her. Actually, Sara had packed a lunch, but most of this was eaten by Carol Ann within ten minutes after they left the station. She had threatened to faint if she was not given food immediately.

Ray sat next to his mother and never shut up from the time the train pulled out. He talked about his various schoolteachers and the days when they used to go to the beach and he recounted things he had done there like rescuing a man from the surf and diving off the end of the pier during a lightning storm: all lies.

"You sound like a damned book report," Carol Ann said, biting into her third sandwich.

But Ray kept on talking, and if his mother looked away or straightened Philip in his seat, Ray would talk louder to keep her attention.

Ben sat separate from the rest of them, three seats behind, by the window. As the train labored through the dark tunnel and then into the light of Park Avenue, he began to be aware of the disaster that was overtaking him. It was like his worst recurring dream where he stood alone on an open plain with the summer sun beating down, and, overhead, huge, black-crested birds circled lower and lower, their talons flashing in the light. In the dream, there was only the sound of wings.

A fat man in a tweed overcoat took the seat next to Ben, puffing and wheezing. He was carrying two bulging shopping bags.

"Hope this train goes to Croton," the man said.

Ben did not hear him.

"Going to a funeral in Croton," the man said, as if this explained everything.

Ben thought that if he could get off the train and run,

the thing that was happening would stop happening and he would be all right: that the circling birds would disappear and he would be on his way to the Planetarium or, at worst, the Botanical Gardens. The tenements flashed by and then the apartment houses and finally there was the Hudson River blazing in the sun. Only it was hard to see through the window where his tears had streaked the glass.

"Got split in half by a blue and white Corvette," the man with the shopping bags was saying. "Never knew what hit him."

Ben was vaguely aware of a pulling on his trousers and Philip's head appeared from under the seat. Ben pulled the little boy into his lap and Philip buried his face in Ben's neck, clinging like a child afraid of the dark. Ben knew that he had guessed what was about to happen, so he held him and spoke to him in soft nonsense words like rickle dickle charlie until Philip finally smiled and eased his grip.

They got into the station at eleven o'clock and they were the only ones to get off. No one was there except the stationmaster; no one to meet them and no taxis in the lot. When Sara discovered this, she sat on a bench on the station platform and put her head into her hands. With this, Winnie began to wail and Carol Ann walked down the platform looking at the posters advertising the Broadway shows, ashamed to be associated with such a group. She vowed then and there that when she grew up she would join the Women's Army Corps and be in charge of an entire platoon who would damn well do what she said and no nonsense.

It was Ben who finally went to the stationmaster and asked how long a walk it was to the School. When they set out, Winnie was still crying, bringing up the rear, dragging her string bag on the ground behind her.

■ ■ ■ ■

MR. ROSE WAS AWAY ON AN ERRAND IN White Plains when they arrived. The psychologist, Mr. Rooney, offered to show them around, but Sara said that if he didn't mind they would sit outside under the trees and wait for Mr. Rose. She fed Philip, breaking a sandwich into bits and giving it to him one piece at a time, but she herself ate nothing. Ray wandered off to the ball field and soon he was part of a game that was going on there. Carol Ann read to Winnie from her stamp-collecting magazine and by sheer force of vocal inflection made the dull articles sound as exciting as adventure stories.

Ben sat with his back to all of them. In his mind he was reviewing the arguments which were already exhausted from too much talk. He could hide from his father (where, Ben, where can you hide? Sara said); his father never really hurt him (not true, you had to stay in the hospital for three days, Ben); it had been his own fault—he had done something to provoke Steve. He would try to do better. What had he done? she wanted to know, and he had searched desperately for a reason. Sworn at him, he said at last. Bad words, from the street. Oh, Ben, she had replied, why did you do it?

■　■　■　■

IN THE END THE COURT HAD INTERVENED and ended all the talk. This, even though Ben swore to them that he had fallen on the fire escape and done the injuries to himself, had repeated the story a hundred times in the same way so there would be no doubt in their minds. It was the slippery soles of his new shoes—they could see for themselves. Why was he on the fire escape? they asked over and over. Fooling around, he said, all the guys fool around there.

"He's been in here before," said the young doctor, glowering over the rim of the chart.

"Sure has," Steve said. "Damned if I don't think the kid is accident-prone."

"Accident-prone?" the young doctor said.

"You know, doc, a need to punish himself," Steve said. The young doctor snorted.

Before the court hearing, Steve had gone back to sea. To the South Pacific, he announced, and he had made Winnie laugh doing an imitation of the hula-hula.

Even Ben, watching, had to smile.

"You take it easy, now," Steve had said to Ben, clapping him on the shoulder. At that moment Ben had seen his mother's face, like a child waiting for a present that might not come. "And stay off those damned fire escapes." Steve had laughed, not as though he had made a joke, but as if he, and Ben too, believed the story.

So he was gone again and the house was quiet, and until they were told that they must appear in court, it was like it was before: as though Steve never existed.

Sara decided that Ray must go too, to keep Ben company, and the authorities had agreed. Ray had not said much. He pulled his mouth into a grimace and tried to think of some questions to ask, but his mind went blank, as it always did in hard times, like during math tests or if he had to speak before the class. Anyway, he was flunking most of his subjects, as he had in every school he had been in, and as usual, the only way seemed to keep moving, backing off and moving like a prize fighter, in an attempt to stay alive.

"Why?" Winnie had said. "Why, why, why, why, why?" Her mother took her into her lap to soothe her. "Just for a while," Sara said. But what Winnie meant was why couldn't she go too! Sara had to laugh when she finally got this out between sobs, and for a moment she was tempted to send them all, even Philip, get them out so that she could relax, so that she would not have to worry every goddamned moment of every goddamned day. Maybe *then* he would get a job in the city and stay with her and they could start a new life together—after all these years.

Carol Ann had looked up from a book she was reading on tropical fish as though Sara's thought had penetrated her mind. On her face was a scolding look, Sara noticed, as though Carol Ann were the mother and she the child.

"Did you say something," Carol Ann had said.

"No," Sara answered.

"Winnie makes so blasted much noise," Carol Ann said, "you can't hear yourself think."

"She's upset," Sara said.

Carol Ann narrowed her eyes and stared at her mother. "So who isn't?" she said. And then, glancing back at her book: "It says here that the Spanish hogfish, which inhabits the waters off the coast of Florida, is also known as the ladyfish. Isn't that a riot?"

■ ■ ■ ■

AS THEY SAT UNDER THE TREES WAITING for Mr. Rose to return, Sara watched Carol Ann reading about her latest interest: stamps. She makes fences out of her books and her pronouncements, Sara thought, shutting out the uncertainties of her life with a barricade of crisp, orderly words that give her time to regroup and go on. This child will make it—this one will toil and tidy and organize and probably arrange the details of her own funeral. Winnie, on the other hand, was the one who worried her. Winnie sitting there, her eyes still damp, listening spellbound to Carol Ann's philatelic readings, the perennial sucker, whose only defense was to drown her opponent in tears. Sara could see her with a succession of men, all standing by wringing their hands until the sounds of her wailing drove them away. Winnie, the one most like her in her inability to cope.

"How long will we have to stay?" Ben was beside her, his voice a whisper.

"A few months," she said, "until things work out."

"How will that happen?"

"Well," she said, "I'm going to have some long talks with your father."

"It won't do any good," Ben said.

"When he realizes the harm he is doing you, I'm sure . . ."

"Oh shit," Ben said.

"Ben, he will kill you if I let you stay."

Carol Ann looked up from her book. Her eyes were wide for a moment, and then she said to Winnie: "Do you know that some people actually frame stamps and hang them on the wall?"

■ ■ ■ ■

JULIE SAT SHIVERING ON THE BED UNTIL
it grew light and she could see the silhouette of her
mother against the sky. All night she had been thinking
that her mother might be dead. She had seen dead people
before, but all of them in the street—one shot to death by
a policeman, and two run over by cars—but there had
been blood and excitement and people crowding around
giving their versions of how it had happened. She did
not know if it was possible to die sitting bolt upright in
a chair by the window and she was afraid to find out.

The boys had not come home, or the Man either, for
that matter. If the Man had been there, things would
have been humming by now. There would be bacon
frying on the stove and the coffee would be made, and
he would have made her mother get up from the chair
and go wash herself.

"Get your sweet ass up," he would have said, and she
would have grumbled, but she would have done it and
after a while they would hear her singing as she splashed
the water over herself.

"Mama, you wake up now. It's time," Julie said.

Her mother was facing away from her, out the
window, and Julie was afraid to go closer.

"Come on now," she said, her voice rising. She was
afraid that if she touched her mother, she would turn to
dust. She began to cry, without making a sound, as she

had learned to do years ago: to yell and scream inside and let the tears come inside so that no one would notice.

"Now, Mama," she said, choking. "Now, Mama, you come on now." She paced up and down the living-room floor, not knowing what else to do with the rising anxiety that threatened to explode her chest, to splatter her in a million pieces all over the wall.

Finally she could stay in the room no longer and she ran into the street. She would find the Man and bring him back. That was the only thing to do.

She was lucky. She found him within five minutes, hanging on the tail end of a garbage truck, together with another man. As the truck roared by, he shouted something to her and waved. She began to run.

She could not remember running as fast as she did that day. It was like the pictures she had seen of Olympic runners, their muscles bulging, their feet barely touching the surface of the earth. She vaulted everything in her way: a sleeping dog, a drunk, a burned-out mattress, and she prayed that the light at the intersection would turn red and hold the truck until she could catch it. The light did turn, but the truck roared through, honking its horn, disappearing around the corner.

She walked slowly back through the streets, aware that she was hungry, that it was getting hot again, and that perhaps they had come for her mother in a long black panel truck.

When she got back to the apartment house, a crowd

had gathered across the street and a police car was pulling up. The cop got out and looked up with the crowd to the top floor. Julie saw her mother standing in the window. She was shouting in a stranger's voice, with mixed-up words, causing a hush in the street, causing the cop to remain where he was, scratching his head.

Gone, everybody goddamned gone. Was that what she was saying? She sounded like the dog Julie had seen trapped on the subway tracks with the train bearing down.

And then the furniture came flying out the window, crashing into the street and on the roofs of the parked cars. First came the kitchen chairs, most of them already broken before making their flight to the street, and the green pillows from the couch, and then the dishes, one by one, going splat on the sidewalk, and then the blanket, which billowed out and caught on the fire escape, and finally three worn winter jackets. The woman's plight had not moved the crowd, but the sight of the automobiles being smashed enraged them and they shouted orders and obscenities and even suggested that she solve her problem by jumping.

When her mother stopped throwing things, Julie knew it was because the apartment was empty.

That day they took her mother to the psychiatric ward for observation, and later, when someone found Julie sitting on the stairs staring at the wall, the cops took her to the Children's Shelter.

■ ■ ■ ■

THAT WINTER BEN SPENT MOST OF HIS TIME
traveling from the School to Brooklyn. He could not
adjust to the dormitory, to sleeping among strangers, to
living with a couple named Dave and Wilma, who insisted he call them Pop and Mom, and to the painful lack
of privacy. Although he was not permitted to go home
except once a month, he went anyway, hitchhiking down
the Parkway or hopping the train, hiding out from the
conductor.

At first Sara seemed glad to see him. "Who's there?"
she would call when he would arrive in the middle of the
night. "Who's there?"

"It's Ben."

"Oh, Ben!" And she would open the door and gather
him in her arms, warm with sleep in her old bathrobe.
"You shouldn't be here, you know." And they would
sit at the kitchen table talking for the rest of the night
until it got light enough for him to travel back. When
Sara would call the School to tell them where he was,
they would scold her and say that she must be firm with
the boy. Otherwise, he would think she wanted him to
be home rather than at the School. Well, she did, but
who was there to tell this to. Of all of them, she felt the
greatest loss over him. He had been too close for her to
separate him without feeling she had actually lost a part
of her physical self. At night she would rouse from a

dream, her random thoughts grief-tinged before she was even fully awake, and remember that he was not in his bed.

The house had changed. With Ben and Ray gone, the little girls had become almost sedate. At first Carol Ann had tried to take charge, bossing Winnie and Philip and even Sara. Winnie, instead of crying as she had in the past, began to turn away from her sister, cutting her off with a supercilious remark, until finally Carol Ann gave up.

"You're all a waste of my time," Carol Ann announced one day, and from then on, she disappeared into her stamp collection or her scientific magazines. Sara watched this abdication with sadness. She wanted to tell Carol Ann that it was all right for her to be the boss, that, God knows, they needed a boss in the house, but she said nothing.

With Ben gone, Philip grew even more pale and thin. He stood for hours at the window, absorbed by a ray of sun striking a chrome car mirror, blinded by the star of light it made. By rocking slightly on his heels, he could change the star into a thousand different blinding shapes. Sara put him in a special class in school, but the noise and the activity of the other children frightened him and he sat silent and alone. She took him to the doctor, finally, who found his pulse, blood pressure, and his chemistries to be normal, but he did not like the boy's waxen color and his listless manner. Has he suffered some kind of a loss? the doctor wanted to know. Yes, Sara said. The doctor suggested putting him in the hospital for observation and to run more tests, but Sara took him home, knowing he would die if she did this.

That night she took the little boy in her arms and held him in her lap, although his legs were almost long enough to touch the floor.

"Would you like to go and live with Ben at the School?" she said.

"Yes," he said, so softly she was not sure at first that she had heard. Then Philip looked at her for the first time in months and smiled. I will lose them all, one by one, she thought.

■ ■ ■ ■

ROONEY, THE SCHOOL PSYCHOLOGIST, FELT that Philip should not live in the same cottage with his brother. He had studied the records carefully and found what he called a pathological interdependence between the two which must be pruned out so that each of them could grow more normally. He told this to the staff, and they all nodded in agreement, impressed that Rooney could make such a decision even before Philip arrived on the scene. Their approval was a comfort to him. Lately he had come to doubt himself, taking the mean things the children said personally, sitting in his office on late winter nights trapped in his own fantasies of success—to publish, to teach, to go on TV and become a household word. But then, as the fantasies soured and the office grew cold, he would drag himself home, angry that his attempts to love and to improve fell on such deaf ears.

"The autistic child needs to learn the boundaries of himself," he had said to the staff. Mr. Rose, the director, made notes, and for a wild, irrational moment, Rooney wondered if Rose might secretly embroider this on a pillow, since he was such a collector of credos and over-simplifications.

He hated Rose, the mediocrity of the man with his pretense of goodness and cheer, hated his stupidity and the fact that he was totally lacking in qualification for the job he held. And yet he held it: Rose was the boss and he was the hired hand. It was Rose's cheeriness that the board of directors found irresistible. If the adults are happy, Rose had told them, the children will be happy. Another Roseian false equation, but when Rose spoke to them, they smiled and felt the ship was in good hands. With him, however, the board smelled his sourness. They listened to his reports, sensing the validity of them, but he often thought his presence was like bad-tasting medicine—a necessary evil.

Philip's attachment to his brother interested Rooney as much as it repelled him. When the child was brought to the School, he asked to see him. It was a dark day and snowing and the boy and the mother came into the office leaving puddles of melting snow on his carpet (God, would he ever get over minding that!), the child hanging back, almost hidden in the folds of his mother's coat. Rooney was not prepared for the physical beauty of the woman or her diffident manner, both with him and with the boy. Had he wished her to be a big, strident woman whom he could blame? He sent for Ben. And when the older boy came into the room, flushed from running, Rooney saw the tripartite merge before his eyes: the son into the mother, and the child into the boy, as though none of them could be complete without the others. Rooney groaned to himself. The textbooks had failed him again.

■ ■ ■ ■

THAT NIGHT, PHILIP LEFT THE COTTAGE HE had been assigned to and wandered around in his pajamas in the snow until he found Ben. He crawled shivering into bed with his brother and lay sobbing and shivering for an hour in Ben's arms until he fell asleep.

■ ■ ■ ■

THE SPRING WAS LONG AND COLD. BEN'S
fear of the School calmed within him and turned slowly
to hate. The routine ground him down—up at the same
hour, down at the same hour, off to the classrooms, re-
peating the same menu week after week. Instead of be-
coming a part, he became a separate, unable to laugh at
Dave's jokes, feeling nothing when Wilma put her hand
on his shoulder. He continued to run away.

"You're going to get yourself in trouble." Dave spoke
slowly, smiling as if it were not really his concern. "If
Mr. Rose hears about this, you'll be grounded."

"How would he hear?" Ben said.

"I might have to tell him," Dave said.

It was the way Dave smiled that was the tip-off—a
slow, preoccupied smile that indicated his mind was
somewhere else, playing with another possibility. Ben
had made a note of it: once, when a boy had lost control
at the table and had to be taken, screaming, into another
room, Dave had picked him up and carried him off as if
they were going on a picnic, as though the violence of
the child touched the man and brought him to life. Ben
tried to tell his mother.

"I think there's something wrong with Dave," he said.

Her face grew pale. "What? Did he hurt you?"

"No. He didn't hurt me."

"Oh well then," she said, dismissing it quickly, "so

long as he doesn't hurt you." They had said no more about it.

That spring he had found out about Madeline. Odie had told him. "Screwed by her own pa-pa," Odie said. "Screwed and pursued."

They were in the gym shooting baskets, and Ben jumped high for a hook shot and missed. He wanted Odie to say more, but he was reluctant to ask. He needn't have worried. Odie sensed a good audience in Ben.

"Started in on her when she was three," Odie said, sending a line drive at the board which spun back against the rim and in. "They didn't catch him until Madeline was eight years old. Ain't that a blast?" He dribbled the ball as if he were being chased by a swarm of bees.

"Where was her mother?" Ben said.

"Who the hell knows?" Odie shouted. "Probably drunk." He arched the ball high in the air and it seemed to hang there from a string. "Probably balling somebody else. Who the hell cares where she was." Odie had never seen his own mother and had little good to say on the subject of parents of either sex.

"Man," he said, as the ball whooshed through the basket. "Man, I got a project that will lay you out. You want to hear?" For the next ten minutes, Odie told him how he planned to steal six basketballs, all at one time, out of the local sporting-goods store.

Madeline's place was on the front steps of Reese

Cottage. She was as permanent there as any gargoyle, even in cold weather. Then she would bundle up in her coat and mittens and read her movie magazine. Sometimes she was known to sit there even in the rain, holding an umbrella over her head as she read. She read about the stars as thoroughly as the social workers read the histories of the children at the School. She knew their birthdates, their favorite songs, the content of their petty quarrels. By living with the stars, she could avoid the petty quarrels inside the cottage, avoid the apathy of the cottage mother and the emptiness of herself.

When Ben first came to see her, she knew he had come to stare. All the new children did when they found out she had been repeatedly raped. "I am a regular Disneyland," she had said once, surprised at her own levity.

But, despite her bravado, she hung her head when Ben came to look at her. Then he had said: "My father did the same thing to me."

"You're kidding," she said. She put down the magazine and looked at him. "What's your name?" She made him sit down and in a moment she had him talking about his own father and Brooklyn and the fact that his brother Ray would probably be moved from the School to a foster home. That afternoon he told her practically everything he knew, and while he was telling her, she began picking over him like a monkey mother, removing bits of lint and loose button strings and then starting on his person, first squeezing a blackhead out of his neck and holding it up for him to admire. After a while they walked down by the railroad tracks, and it was then, on that first day of their meeting, that they decided to make their own house out of a piano crate.

"We have a beautiful river view from here," Madeline said. "I may plant a garden. How about some long-stemmed American Beauty roses? Julie Christie adores them."

"How about radishes?" Ben said.

Madeline sighed. "When we lived in the big house with the wide lawns, we had a full acre of American Beauty roses," she said, "and a gardener to tend them."

Ben knew that she was lying, but he knew also that he could not challenge her. The stories and the movie magazines were what held her together.

"We will have to make this place more homey," she said. "A few color coordinates would help." She took his hand and they walked up the hill through the brush and into town. She took him to a hardware store and made him talk to the man who ran the place while she stole a roll of Con-Tact paper, a can of shell-pink paint, a small paintbrush, and a flashlight. She amassed these things without arousing the slightest suspicion on the part of the man, and when she was finished, she stood in the doorway and cleared her throat, indicating to Ben that it was time to go.

"You were pretty cool in there," Ben said. Madeline barely heard him. She was thinking of her decorating scheme.

The next day after school, the two of them went straight to their house by the river. On one of the walls Madeline attached the Contact paper, and on the other she painted roses with the shell-pink paint.

"We forgot a padlock," she said. "Run up and get one."

"I don't have any money," Ben said.

"Of course you don't," she said pleasantly.

"Why do we need a padlock anyway?" he said, trying to fake her out.

She laid her paintbrush down and scowled at him. All her sweetness seemed to have vanished.

"Go on," she said. "You've got to start sometime."

The man seemed to remember him from the day before and asked him if he could be of help.

"I'm just looking around," Ben said.

There was no one else in the store but the two of them. Ben went to the tool department and began to examine the screwdrivers, weighing each one in his hand as if he were looking for a perfect balance. Maybe he should buy one of these—as a cover. He had to laugh at himself. If he bought the screwdriver, he might as well buy the padlock instead. Except he had no money. And that would be cheating. Madeline would find him out.

The man put down his newspaper and looked at the boy.

"You want something in a screwdriver?" he said.

Ben jumped. "No, no," he said. His voice was too high, he thought, a giveaway. He had stolen things before, mostly fruit and candy from stands on the street. But he had never been caught, and on the street he could always run, or drop it, or both. Here he felt closed in, as though he had a chain around his leg, with the other end tied to the man. He moved on to the electrical-wiring department.

"You live at the School?" the man said.

"No."

"Oh," the man said, "I thought you did."

Ben spent fifteen minutes looking at the various plugs and extension cords and implements for stripping and splicing, and finally the man walked across the room and joined him.

"You're sure you're not from the School?" he said.

"I'm sure."

"That girl you were with yesterday, she's from the School."

"What girl?" Ben was beginning to sweat and he wiped his hands on the back of his pants.

"Pretty little thing. Reminds me of my grandniece."

Next, Ben thought, the man was going to say that Madeline had stolen things and that he was going to call the cops. Ben had to get out, but his feet wouldn't move.

Instead, he began to talk: quickly and in a businesslike tone, which surprised the man and seemed to change the whole atmosphere.

"What I'm really interested in is a padlock," Ben said. "A good strong padlock that can't be busted open."

The man smiled. "Why didn't you say so?" he said. He turned to lead the way to another part of the store, and as he did, Ben slipped a lamp socket into his pocket.

"Not bad," Madeline said when he returned. She emptied out his pockets onto the floor of their house. In addition to the lamp socket and the padlock, there was a magnifying glass, a box of kitchen nails, a pair of scissors, and a mirror.

"The mirror is for you," he said, ducking his head.

"Good," she said in her practical voice. "There's only one problem."

"What's that?"

"You got the padlock, but you forgot the key."

Ben groaned and held his head in his hands. He knew she would make him go back for the key. He knew also that she wouldn't even let him wait until the next day to get it.

■ ■ ■ ■

BY APRIL, BEN HAD BECOME FAIR AS A SHOP-
lifter, urged on by Madeline's decorating impulses and
Odie's unsolicited advice and encouragement. He had
had two fights, both of which he lost, with bigger boys in
his cottage, but by virtue of his having fought well, they
let him alone. He saw less and less of Ray after the first
few trips they made home together. Ray lived with the
older boys and had become a pet of theirs, allowed in
their games and their delinquencies, receiving praise he
had never gotten before. And although the brothers saw
each other every day, passing back and forth across the
grounds or on their way to school, they spoke less and
less, until finally they were almost strangers.

And Ben thought of home. In the classroom, as the
teacher's voice droned on and on, he thought of his
mother, wondered what she was wearing, wondered
what she had made for breakfast. He even convinced
himself that he missed Winnie and Carol Ann. Instead of
the longing growing less in him as the time passed, it
became more intense, until he could feel it in the pit of
his stomach from the time he woke up in the morning
until he went to bed. Homesick and growing sicker.
Then, in order to tolerate it, he made a plan. He would
leave the School on the Fourth of July weekend. In-
stantly he felt better. With this decided, the other boys
with whom he lived became like people he might see in

a train station, people he would not have to contend with for more than a brief time.

Madeline sensed the change in him.

"You look like the weight of the world has been lifted off your shoulders," she told him.

He was down on his knees behind their piano crate planting radish seeds they had stolen from the five-and-ten.

"Yeah," he said. "Well, I'm getting the hell out of here."

"Oh, sure," she said. "That will be the day."

She towered above him, her arms crossed like a Cossack's, and he noticed that she had stopped smiling. He wished he liked her better. He wished she weren't so fat. He wished she weren't fifteen, or that he weren't eleven and that he didn't need her to boss him around. He wished that she didn't wear so much of that damned Evening in Paris perfume. It made his eyes sting.

"Everybody lies about leaving this place," she said, leaning over to take a twig out of his hair, "and they never do."

"Shut your friggin mouth," he said, jumping to his feet. On the side of the hill, he was as tall as she was, and it gave him courage. "And get your goddamned hands off of me," he said, his voice growing shrill. "Always picking on me like I got lice!"

He saw her eyes go blank. He had seen this look on the faces of stray dogs on the street in the wintertime. He had hit her where she lived and he was sick about it, but he couldn't stop. "Why don't you pick on somebody your own age?" He was screaming and he knew that it was not him, that it came from another source, and he wanted to beat her in the face with his fists. It was not like his fights with the boys in the cottage or with Ray, but something worse that he could not stop. He turned and ran down to the tracks and to the station a mile away, not stopping once for breath, or to look back, trying to get the look of Madeline's face out of his mind. When the train came, he went to Brooklyn.

By the time he got to Brooklyn, it was dark and a light rain was falling. He ran the two blocks and up the five flights without stopping for breath, and he pounded on the door as if the cops were after him. From the Ruizes' apartment came the sound of the Spanish radio station and the smell of beans cooking. He pounded again. They were home, because he had seen the lights in the window from the street. He heard a voice which sounded like Winnie's, and then someone else, he couldn't tell who. Finally the door opened a crack, but the chain was on.

"Who is it?" Carol Ann's voice.

"Me. Ben." He wondered why she whispered.

"Wait a minute."

The door closed and she was gone. What the hell was going on, he thought. He started pounding again, and in a minute Carol Ann was back.

"Mama says for you to go back to the School," she said.

"What?" What the hell was she saying?

"Go back!" And she shut the door in his face.

It was a nightmare, he thought. He was dreaming at the School, and now he must wake himself and go to Brooklyn and find out what the trouble was.

Inside the apartment, there was only silence. He put his ear to the door, but he heard nothing more. Over the sound of the radio came Mrs. Ruiz's voice. Was she singing? No. Mr. Ruiz yelled something at her. Ben pounded again and rattled the knob and the sweat poured down his sides and made a pool above his belt.

The door opened at last and there stood his mother. She was wearing a purple dress, one that he had never seen before. He did not like it. For some reason he noticed that her hair was longer, longer than he had ever seen it, and although it looked beautiful to him, he knew that soon she would have it cut back to the old way. She stood looking at him, her expression so painful that it was as if she were making up a face for him to laugh at.

"You must go back, Ben," she was saying, and she reached out and touched his hair.

"Let me in a minute." He tried to push open the door, but it grated against the chain.

"I can't," she said. "He's here."

"Who? Who?" He felt himself reeling. She could not turn him away. She could not do it. Overhead, he thought he heard the whirring sound of a bird.

"Your father arrived this afternoon."

"I've got to tell you about the Fourth of July," he said irrationally. "I mean, it won't take long, and I've got to tell you!" He was beginning to shout.

She started to cry. "Wait a minute," she said, and disappeared from the slit in the door. He leaned against the jamb. Maybe he had gotten into the wrong building. Maybe his mother was really in the building next door.

"Ai ai ai ai," cried Mrs. Ruiz, as a guitar played an arpeggio in the background.

When his mother came back, she was still crying. She took his hand and placed a five-dollar bill in it.

"Here," she said, "take the train. I will call you tomorrow."

"You see," he began, "you see, the Fourth of July is on a weekend." He spoke as if he hadn't heard her. "I'll be coming home for good then."

"Quickly," she whispered. "I think he woke up!"

"That's okay, then? Can I plan on the Fourth of July?"

"Yes!" she said. "Hurry. Go straight back."

"Promise?"

"Promise," she said.

She would have promised him the moon.

■   ■   ■   ■

AT FIRST, DAVE POLISHED HIS CAR BEHIND
the laundry, but later, when he noticed Madeline sitting
on the steps of Reese Cottage reading her movie magazines and exposing her fine, white inner thighs, he moved
his work to the front of the gymnasium, well within her
view. For a while she pretended not to notice him, but
he knew she was watching and he waited. It took two
polishing sessions, but finally she looked up and scowled.
The next day he wore his white cashmere, and he leaned
against his gleaming car and waved. She thought he
bore a strong resemblance to Candice Bergen's current
boyfriend. The following week, he asked her to ride
into town with him while he bought cigarettes. She drew
back instinctively, sorry that he had been so quick to
spoil everything, but he laughed and told her to ask her
housemother if she was so worried about it. His easy,
open manner reassured her and she jumped into the car
beside him.

Wilma watched this from the window of Beakman
Cottage and sighed. She calculated that in six weeks they
would be on the road again, looking for another job.

■ ■ ■ ■

BEN DREAMED OF THE DETAILS OF GOING home. He savored it like candy. His mother would come for him and together they would stroll around the grounds. He would take her to the gymnasium and the classrooms and introduce her to his friends. To Odie and Julie. And maybe Madeline. Well, maybe not to Madeline. He could not make up his mind. He thought of showing his mother their house down by the tracks, but decided against it. What could he tell her about it? But he would take her to see Rooney. Rooney, who sent him formal little notes advising him of his availability to discuss personal problems. They would say goodbye to Mr. Rose. They would take their time and then they would collect Philip and that would be that. On the train ride home, he would fill her in on the details.

Philip continued to sleep with him each night, crossing the grounds in his pajamas when it got dark, regardless of whether or not it was raining, slipping into the cottage as unobserved as a breath of air. The other boys had long since accepted this phenomenon, even helping to warm his feet on the cold nights. To some of them, he became an omen. "Is Philip in yet?" they would ask. Or, if Ben was asleep and the little boy had not yet come, they would decide who would go look for him, to make sure he was all right.

Ben spoke to Philip of their going home.

"Think about the Fourth of July," he would begin, and Philip would stop fidgeting and lie still on his chest.

He told Philip about the first meal they would have at home—everything they wanted: French fries done almost burned, with lots of catchup; spareribs and spaghetti and tunafish salad and chocolate Devil Dogs.

"And root beer?" Philip wanted to know.

"And root beer."

After a while Ben would stop talking and Philip would fall asleep, making a damp spot on Ben's chest from his breath and his slobber.

Only at that time was Ben unable to control the doubts that seemed to seep out of the walls and infest the room. Then he remembered the twisted look on his mother's face and Madeline saying, "Oh sure, that will be the day!" Well, maybe Madeline was right. The more he thought about it, lying there in a dormitory with five other boys, in a place he obviously should not have been put in the first place, the more desolate he felt. Philip stirred and moaned on his chest and it was as though Ben himself had made the sound.

By the middle of May his self-pity had been driven back by a flood of anger, most of it directed at Madeline, whom he taunted for being fat and lazy and for allowing herself to be raped when she was a little girl and for looking at Dave the way she did. It was her own damned fault, he said. One day he hit her across the mouth— neither one of them could remember the reason for it a moment later—and although he was as shocked as he had been when he first yelled at her, he felt a sweet sense of release. She began to cry, not turned away and by herself crying, but with her arms around him and her tears running down his face. He was startled by the closeness he felt.

"Well now," he said, his voice as gentle as a dove's, "what do we have here?"

"What?" she said, pulling back. There was something in his tone of voice that frightened her and made her run off, leaving him looking after her in surprise. Is something burning? she wondered as she made her way through the harsh grass of the riverbank to the road above. Is there a storm coming? She stopped at the top, breathing heavily, her pale skin flushed and perspired. Below she could see him standing by their shack, watching her, his hands in his back pockets. She made herself review the facts: he was a boy, four years younger than herself. His voice, then—was that it? That smooth silky way he spoke, quite different from his usual hesitant way. She turned and walked toward the town. Well now, she heard her father say as he lifted her onto his knee, what do we have here?

■ ■ ■ ■

ON THE FIRST OF JUNE, ROONEY CALLED BEN to his office to tell him that he was going to be sent to a foster home.

"I can't go," Ben said. "I'm going home to stay on the Fourth of July."

"It's with the McCurdy's," Rooney said, as though he had not heard. "Upstate. Near Beacon. You'll like it there. It's in the country, with animals and room to move in."

"I don't need room to move in," Ben said. "Or animals, either."

"Mrs. McCurdy is a dear," Rooney said. He blinked at Ben as though suddenly he had run out of things to say. Then he got up from his desk to jog his mind and stood staring out at the river. An oil tender was passing and he wished he were on it, going away from this place. It was going to be hard to convince Ben of this move, but it was for the best. He was sure of that. If he wasn't sure, then the boy would sense it and not want to go.

"Ray loves *his* foster home," Rooney said, deciding on another tack.

Ray had been gone for months and the only word Ben had had from him was a scribbled postcard, half of which Ben had been unable to read.

"Good for Ray," Ben said. "But my mother said—"

"You see, in a foster home you will have a nice stable environment—" He had not meant to say such a stilted thing and he bit his lip as if that would bring back the words.

"—she'd take me home. It's all settled."

"Let me tell you about Mrs. McCurdy," Rooney said, trying to infuse his voice with cheer.

"I don't care about her."

"Fine sense of humor," Rooney slogged on, "not an old sourpuss like me." Oh God, what had slipped out now? But Ben looked up and smiled for the first time.

"Maybe you can't help it," Ben said.

Had he won ground, or lost? Rooney wondered. With a boy like Ben, it was hard to tell. But he felt cheered and he went on to describe the foster home with more gusto, despite the fact that he had never seen it, or Mrs. McCurdy either, for that matter. He relied on the foster-home finder for all his information.

"She runs a nice clean home," the foster-home finder had said, but somehow Rooney could not bring himself to share this information with Ben. Instead, he told him that there were cows and geese in the barn and a fireplace in the living room and a pond out in back. He would go to the local school by bus. There were three other foster children, Rooney said, and they all ate together in a large cheery kitchen. Rooney rattled on, knowing that Ben's mind had wandered off. But alas, he could not stop talking, even though he had exhausted everything the foster-home finder had told him and was now improvising on his own.

■ ■ ■ ■

THERE WERE GEESE ALL RIGHT. STANDING wing-tip to wing-tip, they made a flying wedge, sweeping the yard clean of chickens, dogs, cats, and children. The only one not intimidated by them was Mrs. McCurdy, who shooed them with her apron, scolding them fondly as they hissed and arched their necks in mock attack, the pupils of their yellow eyes dilating with excitement.

A stained gray barn stood at one end of the property, one side of it caved in from the fifty years of fierce winter wind and no one to repair it. In the side that still functioned, two Guernsey cows, one of them totally dry and the other giving a thin stream of blue liquid almost devoid of butter fat, stomped and chewed in their stalls. Their old eyes saw little beyond the scope of their mangers, and they had long since learned to bear the humiliation of foster boys pulling painfully at their teats. They were named Dolly and, for some reason, Ranger.

That spring, still gray and cold in late May, found the ground spongy from the thaw, found the animals irritable from the prolonged winter. The cold had driven the mice and moles deep into their burrows, leaving the barn cats thin and anxious and yearning for the sun. It looked as though the sky would never clear.

Mrs. McCurdy met Ben and Miss Bianca, the foster-home finder, in the driveway, a rose-colored cardigan over her shoulders, her arms folded across her breast for warmth. A hard wind blew across the yard, stretching out the new branches of the weeping willows like strands of thin hair.

They had left the School at eight, as though they were going on an all-day trip, and what should have taken an hour stretched into two. Miss Bianca was not the best driver in the world, and from time to time she would stop the car and consult the map, looking as if she were trying to decipher a code, and would end up pulling into a gas station for directions. She talked almost without stopping, speaking to Ben in a slangy way and sprinkling in things she had just learned at social-work school—things she hoped would make him feel more comfortable. She told him about the other foster children who lived with the McCurdys—two of them placed there by the Welfare and the other from the School—but Ben was not listening. He thought only of Philip.

"He must learn to live separate from you," Rooney had said. "Find his own boundaries, establish himself as an entity."

"He can't," Ben had said.

"We will help him," Rooney had replied.

Before he left, Ben talked to Philip night after night, telling him that he would not be gone long, reminding him of the Fourth of July. But the little boy grew totally silent and so soft in Ben's arms that he seemed actually to melt into Ben's skin. It was hard even for Ben to know where Philip stopped and he began.

"In September," Miss Bianca was saying, "you'll go to the local school. It's too late to enroll now."

"I'm going home the Fourth of July," Ben said.

"Well," Miss Bianca said, turning abruptly into the long driveway of the McCurdy farm, "we'll see how you like it here."

Ben did not answer. He had long since written off Miss Bianca.

■ ■ ■ ■

HE SHARED A ROOM WITH WILLIAM, AGED nine, and Peetie, thirteen. These boys had lived in foster homes all their lives. A six-year-old named Andy also shared the room. Andy and William wet the bed and the smell of their urine permeated the curtains, the bedspreads, and the woodwork. Mrs. McCurdy tried to hide the odor with a heavy Lysol spray, but this only made it worse.

"We'll put you by the window," she was saying, and she opened the cardboard cupboard for his belongings. He did not want to look at her, so he put his clothes away and sat down on the bed while she and Miss Bianca chatted.

"He'll like it here," Mrs. McCurdy was saying. Her voice was as heavy as a man's and laced with cheerfulness. "They all come around after a while."

It sounded to Ben like a threat.

■ ■ ■ ■

HE SPENT MOST OF HIS DAYS IN THE BARN. In the attic he found old pieces of harness and hand-wrought implements from a forge and wooden boxes full of rusty bolts and hinges. He found horseshoes and a ring made from a horseshoe nail which fit his middle finger. When she came looking for him, he hid in the haymow. He hated the way she whacked him between the shoulders blades: "Well, boy, it's another day. Rise and shine!" He hated the way she piled his plate with macaroni and potatoes and stood over him, laughing and cajoling him to eat. He hated the three sullen boys with whom he had to sleep, but they were at least away at school during the day. He hated Mr. McCurdy, who appeared only at dinnertime, home from his contracting jobs in his pickup truck, grunting and mumbling over dinner and snoring in front of the TV in the evening.

Oh, Rooney, you are a sonofabitch, he thought.

From the barn, Ben could keep track of the geese. They spent most of their time at the edge of a filthy pond near the back fence. He had tried to pet one of them, but had been attacked by all five—such an awesome attack that he ran to the barn for safety, with the five of them after him, their wings lifted in anger.

■ ■ ■ ■

"YOU CAN CALL ME MOM," MRS. MCCURDY said, after he had been there a week.

He turned and walked off without answering.

"Wait and see," she called after him. "We'll end up being regular lovers!"

■ ■ ■ ■

"I WANT TO CALL MY BROTHER," HE SAID to her one morning.

She was preparing a casserole from rice and ground meat and onions, mixing the ingredients with her hands.

"I don't know about that," she said. "Miss Bianca didn't say you could."

That afternoon he walked four miles to the nearest pay phone. It was a winding road through the gently rolling hills, and only occasionally did a car pass, honking him over to the side. He grew apprehensive in the silent countryside, hooded over by dark gray clouds threatening rain. He had been outside of the city only once before, years ago, when his father borrowed a car from a friend and they all drove to Connecticut to have a picnic. It had been a disastrous day, with the car stalling and finally coming to a standstill on a hot and dusty road (they decided to have the picnic there), and Winnie throwing up all over the back seat.

He found a phone in a gas station, and although he got through to the cottage where Philip lived and somebody was sent out to look for him, Ben ran out of money before they found him. The operator cut him off: with apologies.

When he got back to the farm, it was almost dark. He went directly to the barn and took a can of kerosene which was kept on a shelf behind the door. The geese were on their way to the barn for the night. He was able to separate one of them, cornering it against the back fence. Then he poured kerosene over it and set it on fire. The goose ran shrieking toward the pond, lighting up the yard like a meteorite. It managed to get into the water and its impetus to escape propelled it mechanically around the pond a few times despite the fact that all its feathers had burned away and its brain was dead.

Mrs. McCurdy grew white with rage as the sight of one of her darlings being treated in such a fashion, and she hit Ben across the face until his nose bled.

"You're lucky I don't set you on fire," she said. She threatened to report him to the School and to tell her husband about this atrocity, and finally she sat down in the kitchen with the evening newspaper, turning the pages angrily without reading what was on them.

When her husband pulled into the yard in the pickup, she ran out to meet him. It was hard to say what Mr. McCurdy thought about most things, since he spoke only in grunts and groans. "Arrah," he would say, which was usually positive and could mean "How are you," or "Thanks," or "All right." And he had a variety of "s" sounds, all negative, all derivations of "shit." "Shaaaa," he would explode, if he tripped or hurt himself with a hammer. "Shiiiiiii," if the bath water was too cold.

When he heard about the goose from the shocked lips of his wife, he laughed until the tears rolled down his cheeks. He hated them. They were forever pecking at the tender hairless flesh of his legs, leaving bruises which lasted the winter. He saw them as his wife's troops who would some night overcome him as he slept.

"Oh Jesus," he said clearly, as though he finally had a reason to be understood. "Oh, what I wouldn't have given to see that!" And he wiped his tears and blew his nose with a big red kerchief.

Before Mrs. McCurdy could call the School to report the incident, they telephoned her. It was after dinner and Ben had been sent upstairs without the blessing of the casserole.

"They are on their way to pick him up," she said to her husband. "Something has happened."

Her husband had settled in front of the TV.

"Good riddance!" she hissed.

Watching her go off to the kitchen, her arms held away from her body, her neck arched in indignation, Mr. McCurdy fell into another fit of the giggles.

■　■　■　■

JULIE WILLIAMS HAD BEEN THE FIRST TO see Philip on the tower. She spotted him after she was forced to abandon her chase of the Man, whom she had seen leaving the gymnasium. This time the Man was disguised in a pair of running shorts and a sweatshirt and was wearing dark goggles, the kind ski racers use. He was a fool to think she wouldn't recognize him, regardless of what he tried to hide in, and she was in the process of saying this, muttering to herself as she jogged along, when she saw what looked like a human form at the top of the water tower down by the river. For a moment she thought it might be the Man himself, trying to hide out from her there, and she was halfway down the hill, running through the brush and thinking that finally she had him trapped, when she realized that it wasn't a man at all but a small boy.

The tower was one place the kids at the School stayed away from, especially in the winter, when ice formed on its metal legs, making climbing impossible. There was also a rumor that several people had been killed there, part of a crew sent to repair a leak. At any rate, when Julie saw that it was a boy, climbing slowly and almost at the top, she sat down on the bank to watch. It was late in the day and a strong wind was already blowing, and from somewhere on the top of the tower a loose piece of metal banged and clanged, like the sound from a buoy at sea.

The little boy picked his way delicately up the rusted steel girders, stopping now and then to wipe his hands on the back of his pants. She noticed that he was not wearing a sweater, only a pair of jeans and a blue shirt. He must be cold up there, she thought.

As she watched, her mind drifted back to the Man she had been chasing. Lately he was putting her to more and more rigorous tests—even appearing one day in a lady's dress behind the wheel of a blue Ford convertible. She had begun to wonder if the Man was now in league with

the School, appearing and disappearing only to torture
her, or to punish her for something she had done which
she could not remember. The week before, she thought
she had seen him in a panel truck, and when she had
finally caught up with him (she could now outrun any
boy in the school), he had actually opened the door to
the truck and let her in. Only then did she see that he
was an impostor, and she had had to bite him on the arm
to make him let her out again. Rooney was probably
behind it all, she thought bitterly, shit-ass Rooney with
his runny eyes and his terrible stinking breath!

A gust of wind smashed against the tower and the
little boy clutched the girder with both arms until it
subsided. Then he continued to climb.

Julie did not connect the Man any more with Bernice
or, for that matter, with herself before she came to the
School. Her memory of that time contained no sequence
of events. Bernice remembered was a shadow by a
window, but why she was there and what relationship
she bore to Julie was unclear.

"Try to remember. Try!" Rooney had urged.

"Why?" she had said.

"Well . . ." He had started to say something, but he
was blocked by the ponderousness of his own thoughts
and finally had to leave the sentence hanging.

"What do you think I'd remember?" Julie had said.
She could not resist beating on him a bit. "Maybe that I
was a princess and lived in London, England?"

Rooney had shrugged.

"Oh, Rooney," she had said, "you are such a creep."

And with hangnails, she thought as she watched the little boy pause in his climb and examine his hand. Nearsighted. Nothing to recommend him.

■ ■ ■ ■

THEY DROVE THROUGH THE NIGHT WITH Mr. Ferguson at the wheel and Mr. Rose sitting with Ben on the back seat.

"I don't know what got into him," Mr. Rose said. His voice was petulant, as if anger would keep him from revealing his concern. "He seemed to be making a very good adjustment."

Ben stared out at the dark countryside. He felt as though someone had him around the throat. Certainly Mrs. McCurdy was mad enough to. Or his father. But it was worse than that. With Mrs. McCurdy or his father he would know what to do: run or relax and wait for it to pass, but at the moment it was like suffocating without knowing the source, without being able to see what was after him. Was he dreaming then, the old dream of the birds circling over his head? He looked for a sign in the darkness, some clue as to when and if he might wake up.

■ ■ ■ ■

AT THE BASE OF THE WATER TOWER, IT
looked as if a carnival had come to town. There were
two searchlights of the kind used at supermarket open-
ings. There were seven police cars and a self-appointed
crew of young men in zip-up sports jackets who
patrolled the crowd, warning them away from the
base of the tower. A fire engine stood to one side, waiting for the signal from the police chief to hoist the
ladder. Already three of the young men had climbed the
tower, only to be bullhorned down by the chief when
it seemed certain that the little boy would jump to
avoid them.

It was Rooney's idea, finally, that they get Ben. He
hated concluding this, because it meant that he had
failed in his effort to separate the two boys. But when
he suggested it, the chief nodded. A man-to-man nod
which filled Rooney with pride.

The children from the School gathered on the riverbank. Unlike the townspeople, they showed no emotion.
They sat without speaking through the late afternoon
and into the evening, their chins in their hands, watching,
not going in when they were called for supper. They
looked like the waiting families of men trapped in a mine.
Only Julie Williams left their ranks and milled among
the crowd by the tower. It was she who had reported the
event. She had sat watching Philip until he reached the

top of the tower. She watched him sit down on the narrow ledge, but after a while she grew bored with the scene and wandered into town. On her way back to the School, an hour or so later, she glanced down the bank and, seeing that he was still sitting there, decided someone should know about it. She decided to tell Rooney, more to confound him than anything else, and she was surprised and a little pleased when he immediately picked up the phone and in a quiet voice called the police. He then thanked her for telling him and strode out of his office to attend to the matter, without once fumbling or saying anything stupid. Not bad for a shit-head, she was forced to admit.

When the car pulled into the crowd, there was a ripple of excitement. Who was this boy? The rumors flew. The chief of police waved everyone back and put a paternal arm over Ben's shoulder. He tried to calm the boy by keeping his voice matter-of-fact.

"Now what we'd like for you to do," the chief said, "is talk to him on the horn."

"That will scare him," Ben said.

Ben felt his heart crashing against his ribs and he was afraid he was going to faint or shit his pants or something terrible like that. Above him he could see the oval of Philip's face against the dark sky. The tower seemed to sway as he looked at it, and he wondered if he could keep from passing out. His stomach churned. Then he saw Julie Williams in the crowd. She was looking straight at him and he could see the sweat glistening across the bridge of her nose. She grinned at him and winked, and that did it. Her idiotic gesture suddenly settled him and he knew he would be all right.

He turned down a number of other suggestions the chief made. One was to persuade Philip to jump into a net, another to go with a fireman on the end of the ladder and pluck him off his perch.

"I'll climb up and get him," Ben said.

The chief shook his head. He could not risk one boy's life for another's foolishness. Ben leaned against the car, keeping his eyes on Philip. Philip was standing with his back to the tower, watching the running light of a helicopter moving like a fat lazy star across the sky as it patrolled the river. The police chief took Rooney aside, and Rooney squatted down on the ground next to Ben, talking with him in a quiet way. Julie Williams came out of the crowd and edged near them, and when Rooney looked up and nodded to her, indicating that she was a part of them, she walked over to Rooney and leaned her elbow on his shoulder while he talked to Ben. She is touching me, Rooney thought—my God, she is actually leaning on my shoulder!

In a few minutes, Rooney told the chief that he thought Ben should be allowed to climb the tower and get his brother.

■ ■ ■ ■

THE DAY SHE DIDN'T COME FOR HIM, WHICH was the Fourth of July, Ben waited an hour in the reception hall. Then he went down by the river, trying not to look at the tower, taking his suitcase with him, being careful not to get his shoes muddy, watching that the brambles didn't tear his new suit. It had been her idea to meet him at the School.

When he had tried to telephone her, a voice had interrupted and said: "This is no longer a working number." He did not believe this, but thought instead that he had mixed things up and that his mother really meant for him to take the train home. Before he got on the train, he climbed a tree on the riverbank and tied his suitcase among the branches. He knew of course that he was not coming back this way, but the suitcase was too heavy to lug on the train, especially since he would be traveling without money.

It was daylight before he got to Brooklyn. He banged on the door with his fist. Maybe they were asleep, he thought. The Fourth of July, they would sleep late. He banged harder.

A woman in a nightgown wearing thick spectacles opened the door and looked at him down the long plane of her nose.

"Yes?" she said. "Yes?"

The woman was no help. She and her husband had moved in three weeks before, she said, and she knew nothing about the previous tenant. When Ben asked if he could come in and look around, she was skeptical, but then she remembered that her husband was home, asleep, and there was no need to be afraid. Besides, the boy looked harmless enough.

He went from room to room, put off by the change in furniture, by the change in the smells that he remembered. The woman followed him closely, making sure he didn't steal anything, asking him questions which he didn't bother to answer. He thought that somewhere in the apartment he would find a clue as to where she had gone, an address, some kind of giveaway, a map saying proceed to Babylon, thence to the treasure. When he opened the door to the bedroom where the woman's sleeping husband lay, she told him he had better go. He was beginning to make her nervous.

As he went through the streets looking for her, he kept thinking of Philip. He could not think of Philip's face without hearing the sound of the wind screaming through the girders. Had Philip been trying to say something? Like sometimes when he tried to explain about a piece of junk he found in the gutter it would take him an hour to get a sentence together. "But you see . . ." he would start. "But you see . . ." The wind had blown the words out across the river.

"Was she redheaded?" the vegetable man was saying.
"Yes, that's her."

He had told Philip to stay put, not to move. Had Philip heard, over the wind?

"She hasn't been around for weeks," said the vegetable man. "You a friend of hers?"

It was true that they had gone to the White Tower and sat side by side eating a hamburger, and then walked home together, and that night he had not felt entirely like her son. He remembered the way her hair curled at the back of her neck, as Philip's did. He had always resented that Philip looked like her in other ways—you have your mother's eyes, they would say to Philip—while he seemed to favor his father.

■　■　■　■

"YOU STAY PUT!" HE HAD NOT STOPPED for breath as the police chief had advised, but climbed as quickly as he could, the floodlights playing over the girders. Had the light blinded Philip?

■ ■ ■ ■

BEN WENT FINALLY TO THE GRAVEYARD TO think. He sat on Elizabeth Addison's grave and tried to put Philip out of his mind and figure out where his mother had gone. Lost Mountain, Wyoming? She had laughed: "What would we do in Lost Mountain, Ben?" None of this would have happened if we had gone then, he thought. Even the old men in the red and orange moving van who would have taken them there might have found jobs that would have been easier on their backs.

He watched a man placing a flag on a nearby grave. It was probably his brother who died in the war, Ben thought. His brother? No, his father. His father who wore a hat with a flat brim and fought in the trenches in World War I. Or was it his brother, after all?

■ ■ ■ ■

IF HE HAD JUST STAYED PUT, EVERYTHING would have been all right. The question was, of course, was Philip trying to jump toward him or away from him? Philip had stretched out his arms, but was it a gesture for Ben to take him down from his terrible perch, or did he think, as he sometimes did, standing on a rock in the park, flapping his thin arms up and down, that he could fly? Where had she buried him?

■ ■ ■ ■

BY MID-AFTERNOON THE GRAVEYARD WAS full of people, some having come to decorate the graves, some to eat a picnic lunch and cool themselves under the trees. On all sides was the constant explosion of firecrackers, like the dregs of a small war, punctuated from time to time by the sound of a garbage can blown into the air by a Hong Kong rocket. Ben did not hear. He wanted to leave but he did not know where to go, who to look for, what to do. It was as though Elizabeth Addison herself had wrapped her bony arm around his ankle, holding him there.

He became aware that someone was standing over him, casting a shadow on him and the tombstone he leaned against.

"Come on, take it." A woman in a sleeveless print dress was handing him a sandwich, but he could not think of anything to say to her.

"It's not poison, you know!" She laughed, but the laugh had an angry sound to it, as though she already knew he would refuse.

Philip had floated past, out of reach, like a bird riding an updraft, as though he had control of his flight, as though, if he had wanted to, he could have soared over the river and landed on the steep cliffs beyond. Had she buried him here? Sara had not let him come to the funeral. "You have had enough sadness," she had said. At the bottom of the tower where Philip had finally landed, they loaded him into a bag. Like a bag of broken chicken bones for the garbage. He had not flown anywhere, after all, except straight down.

"How about some fruit?" the woman was saying. She bent over him, shaking a peach in front of his nose, the heavy fat of her underarm swaying like a huge white hammock.

Ben looked at her, but he could not seem to understand what she was saying. It was as though his mind was split away from his head and was hanging in a tree somewhere. He took a black marking pencil out of his pocket. *Fuck you Elizabeth Addison,* he wrote on the gravestone.

"What are you doing?" the woman cried. "What in the goddamned hell are you doing, messing up the dead like that!" Her big arms pumped up and down like pistons in her attempt to control her dismay, and she squeezed the peach so hard that the juice ran down her wrist.

Ben started to run.

He knew where the new graves might be, and he went there to check for Philip. There were four fresh ones, one an infant of six months named Rudolph William Zimmer, and three old ladies. Rudolph William Zimmer was probably beaten to death, Ben thought. At the School, Ben had learned that this was a nightly entertainment in some households, whereas before he had thought he was the only one. In his mind he heard the conversation: "Let's go to the movies tonight, dear." "No, let's stay home and beat the baby." Poor Rudolph William. Probably cried too damned loud, Ben thought.

"A sickness," his mother had told him. "He beats you because he can't help himself." Ben had never told her about the other things his father had done to him. He had not known how to say it. But sickness? Was it catching? Like measles? Like the clap? Poor Rudolph William had caught something, all right: his old man's fist right in the ear.

The sky, which had been clouding rapidly, suddenly grew dark and it began to thunder. For a while the firecrackers stopped, as though in deference to the supernoise of the thunder. It would rain soon, Ben thought.

Before they buried him, had they listened carefully to see whether or not he was breathing? Sometimes with Philip it was hard to tell. As he sat on a large monument marked "de Russo," he decided that he could have caught Philip if he had leaned farther out from the girder. But if he had done so, he would have ended up at the bottom of the tower too. Still, it had been up to him.

That night, and for the next three days, Ben searched all the graveyards he could remember: St. John's and St. Michael's and the Lutheran's in Queens; the Trinity Cemetery, where he had played when they lived near the George Washington Bridge; and St. Raymond's and the New Calvary under the Expressway. As he walked through the rows and rows of graves, he began to lose sight of Philip in his mind. It was as though Philip's slobber, which he always felt to be on his chest, had begun to dry up and blow away. By the time he got to the Woodlawn Cemetery in the Bronx, he had forgotten the color of Philip's and his mother's eyes. His father must have come for her, he thought. For her and Carol Ann and Winnie, and by now they would be riding down an interstate highway toward Virginia. If he could intercept them on the highway, he would drag his father out of the car and run a knife through his gut and toss him into a ravine. They would then proceed to Lost Mountain. But in his mind he could see only the tail end of the car going farther and farther down the road until finally it disappeared over the rim of the horizon.

On the evening of the third day, he boarded a passenger train, and when it slowed for the station at the School, Ben decided to jump off and walk up the hill rather than go all the way into the platform. But he miscalculated the train's speed and bounced off his feet onto his head and lay there all night alongside the tracks, slipping in and out of consciousness.

■ ■ ■ ■

WHEN MADELINE FOUND HIM DOWN BY the tracks, he had a deep wound in the side of his head. His eyes were open but he seemed strange and listless.

"Can you walk?" she said. She did not think she could carry him.

He tried to get up, but he fell back. The second time, she put her arms around his waist and got him to his feet. She held him quietly until he got used to standing, and then, step by step, they made their way along the tracks until they came to a path that led to their shack.

"You're going to rest in here for a while," she said. She made him lie down on a blanket and plumped a bright orange pillow under his head.

"I got a few more things while you were gone," she said brightly. "The new manager of the five-and-ten is half blind."

He wished she would shut up. His head was throbbing so that with each pulsebeat he was afraid he would throw up. She took off his shoes and his torn jacket and she wiped his wound with a piece of the jacket fabric which she dipped into a carton of iced Coke.

"You never should have gone to that damned foster home," she said, examining the rest of him for bruises and scratches. Monkey mother, he thought, but her hands were soothing and the pain in his head seemed to be getting less.

"They think they know so much," she said, "planning our lives like we were a bunch of damn-fool idiots! Why don't they leave us alone!" He had never seen her angry before and the fact that her fingers on his head were so gentle even while her voice was rising made him smile up at her.

When she finished her tirade and her search of his skin and bones, she made him eat half of a sandwich which she had hidden in a milk crate. It was stale and dry, but he managed to get it down. Then she read to him from one of her movie magazines—an article on the carryings-on at the Cannes Film Festival—until he fell asleep.

Later on, she woke him and they walked up the bank to the School together. She took him a different way than they usually went, so that he would not have to see the water tower.